BUG

YOU WON'T BEL
OR WHAT'S ABO

SQUIRMSTERS!

They are genetically engineered caterpillars, hungry for human flesh, and bursting loose on a commuter flight to the Pacific Northwest. Their midair feast is about to begin!

TYRANTULA!

They are aggravated arachnids swarming out of the Arizona desert, stirred up by a secret government weapons test. Now the town of Purgatory is about to get a taste of the tarantula's tangy bite!

SHOCKROACH!

They are irradiated, mutated cockroaches, and they don't like loud music. So when Trina Montero and her friend Louis crank the tunes, their apartment building becomes a high-rise magnet for rampaging roaches hungry for more than quiet!

MUTANTS!

When Robbie orders an ant colony complete with eggs from a comic book, things turn scary. The ancient breed of prehistoric people-eaters are bigger, stronger and meaner than any normal ant, and now they're on the loose!

THE BUG FILES

MutAnts!

DAVID JACOBS

sapling

MUT-ANTS!

First published in the UK in 1996 by Sapling,
an imprint of Boxtree Limited,
Broadwall House, 21 Broadwall, London SE1 9PL.

First published in the USA in 1996 by Berkley Books,
published by The Berkley Publishing Group,
200 Madison Avenue, New York, New York, 10016

10 9 8 7 6 5 4 3 2 1

ISBN: 0 7522 0328 2

Printed and bound in Great Britain by
Cox & Wyman Ltd, Reading, Berkshire.

A catalogue record for this book is available from the
British Library.

1

65 Million Years Ago

EARTH WAS ALREADY OLD, BILLIONS OF YEARS old, but life was young. It had only been an eyeblink of cosmic time since life had first come crawling out of the sea.

It was the Age of Reptiles, but there were other forms of life. Nature's workshop was constantly evolving new ones, on every scale, from micro to macro, from small to great.

Nature was a joker. There was no telling which kinds of life-forms would thrive and multiply, and which would go extinct. Size, strength, speed were no guarantee of success. Sometimes, the smallest of the small was more fit to survive than the greatest of the great.

Sometimes, the smallest of the small could be the deadliest of all, particularly in large quantities. For there is greatness in numbers.

It was late one afternoon, in a day of what

would someday come to be known as the Late Cretaceous period, in a place that would someday come to be known as part of something called Ohio.

There was something in the air, some scent of danger. Grazing armor-plated saurians stirred restlessly, pausing, looking up. Not at the sky. The carnivorous, bat-winged pterosaurs weren't even a nuisance to these great armor-plated hulks.

In the south, the earth shook under the tread of the terrible titan, Tyrannosaurus rex.

In this savage world, the most ferocious killing machine was the Tyrant, or so it seemed. So it seemed.

This was a female of the species, a she-rex. She was as big as a steam shovel. Her head was as big as the steam shovel's bucket. Her teeth were daggers, rows of them. Her eyes, the size of sand pails, were wickedly glaring.

She stood on two legs, a mountain of flesh. Clawed forearms, comically small in proportion to the rest of her, made curved hook shapes, held high on her chest. Her slabbed tail was a juggernaut. She stamped and thumped, roaring. She was hungry.

Hissing, tail lashing, she set off in search of a meal. Fierce, fiendish, fearless, like all her kind. Confident in the certain supremacy of the supreme killing machine of the age. No creature existed that did not fear and would not fall to the Tyrant tribe.

She stalked west, across the grassy plain, leaving behind the soft, soggy marshlands. The hunting wasn't so good in the marshes. The muddy ground slowed her down, allowing the prey to escape.

There was much game in the forest. The wall of green was no barrier to the she-rex, who could bull a path through it, wherever she liked.

At the forest's edge, going into or out of it, creatures were momentarily exposed, vulnerable. It was a good place to hunt.

The grazing saurians, turtlelike ankylosaurs and three-horned triceratops, kept a watchful eye on the Tyrant as she crossed to the forests.

The edge of the woods was curved, like a coastline, with "coves" and outcroppings. Where the Tyrant stood, twin wings of woodlands curved around her, like horns.

The woods *clicked.*

The forest was alive with the sound of a million clickings. Millions and millions of little clicking noises, rattlings, and buzzings. Together, they added up to one industrious racket. Busy. Determined. Relentless.

The ground seemed to move under the Tyrant's feet. Something had been moving under them for the last quarter hour, but it had taken this long for awareness of the phenomenon to come to the monster's tiny brain. Yet it wasn't the ground that was moving.

The ground was covered with insects. They were moving eastward, out of the woods. It was a mass exodus. They poured out of the woods, these crawling things, in numbers so great that they carpeted the ground. They fled the woods, moving in the opposite direction as fast as they could.

This meant nothing to the Tyrant, except to draw her attention to the slippery pulp underfoot, a slimy coating of squashed bugs.

She went on toward the woods, uncaring of the outgoing tide of bugs. They meant less to her than the wind.

Now she was fifty yards distant from the forest's edge. The clickings were louder. Clickings and clackings. They didn't come from the bugs. The bugs made their own sound as they swept across the landscape, a dry rustling sound, like acres of dry dead weeds rubbing together.

The click-clacking was something virtually unknown and unheard of in the Age of Reptiles. It was the sound of *industry*.

A breeze lifted, bringing the scent of a strange, alien reek. Sharp, acidic, hateful.

The flight from the woods had become general. Small reptiles, the size of squirrels, cats, and dogs, burst from the underbrush, scuttling across the fields.

At first, there were only a few, but the forest's edge began to give up more and more. Streams of lizards, then a flood.

They exploded out from the woods, fleeing in blind panic.

Nearby, in the wall of the woods, there was a gap, the mouth of a game trail reaching deep into the forest. It was an avenue of escape for the raptors and other similar-sized reptiles.

The she-rex caught sight of motion, swimming up the path. She turned, facing it, standing outlined in the mouth of the trail.

A red tide rolled along the path. It was flat, but covered the width of the path. Behind it lay its coils and columns, stretching out of sight in the forest gloom.

It was like a giant flat snake, a ribbon snake. It was a dusky red color. Copper red. There was something metallic in it, glinting.

Its broad back glinted with diamond-hard points of light, shifting, ever-moving.

It clicked and clacked, rustled and rattled.

The she-rex stepped toward it, into the forest. Her head was as tall as some treetops, but a few paces into the trail, the trees rose high above her.

The Tyrant moved slowly, unwilling to commit herself. Each footfall pounded the earth.

She came to a halt as a heavy acid reek hit her square in the face.

That harsh alien stink, raw, chemical. Stronger than ever. Her eyes burned, watering.

Now the head of the copper-red column was only a stone's throw away.

There was a wet hiss, a giant liquid sigh.

From the copper-red column rose a copper-red mist, a cloud. It drifted down the trail, to the Tyrant. It was a toxic cloud, poison.

The Tyrant's eyes burned, blazing with blinding pain. Her nostrils, moist tender membranes, burned where touched by the poison mist. She labored, panting, vision blurring.

Things dropped down on her from above, from the treetops, long airy strands of copper-red stuff.

Long lacy streamers of the stuff floated on the air, drifting, lazily spiraling downward. They were like giant strands of copper-colored cobwebs.

For all that they seemed to be at the mercy of the breeze, they managed to twist and turn so as to fall on the Tyrant. Strand after strand attached themselves to the boulder-sized head. When they were secure, they broke up into little bits. Very little bits.

Each bit was . . . an *ant.*

The ant, a recent evolutionary development,

had only been around for some few hundreds of millions of years.

It was a very fit form of life. Ants were well adapted for the microworld, while their social behavior gave them a strength and impact greater than their numbers. Which were legion.

The individual ant was part of something greater, the colony. It would give its life for the colony.

This powerful instinct was a recipe for success.

They were swarm raiders. They foraged in groups. The colony was mobile, traveling across the landscape in a mass. It would settle in an area, pick it clean, then move on.

These copper-red ants were forerunners of what would ultimately evolve into today's swarm-raiding species, variously known as driver, legionary, and army ants. They would someday be scientifically classified as *Myrmex hoplitae. Myrmex,* for the Greek root word for ant. *Hoplitae,* for hoplites, the heavily armored infantry of the Bronze Age Greek kingdoms, the Age of Heroes.

Each hoplite ant was the size of its descendant the wasp—minus the wings. Its segmented body looked like it was forged from red copper. Its burnished helmeted head sported a pair of vicious hook-shaped mandible jaws, their curved inner edges jagged and saw-toothed, designed for ripping and tearing.

They were not its only, or even its most deadly, means of attack defense.

The ant's body comprised three parts: the head, thorax, and abdomen. In the tip of the tail of the swollen, teardrop-shaped abdomen lay a curved sting, like a wasp's. The stinger was hollow and supplied by venom sacs.

The hoplite was not one of those insects, like certain kinds of bees, that stings once, and dies doing so. Like wasps, it could sting again and again, draining its venom, without damaging itself. And sting again it would, at the slightest provocation.

It had a variation on this defense that was devastating, especially in groups. The hoplite could empty its venom in one burst, squirting it out the hollow-tipped stinger.

A snoutful of toxic venom could disable an insect attacker. Done in mass, by a swarm of the raider ants, the sudden discharge of so much venom into the air created a toxic cloud, a poison mist.

The ants would attack anything in their path, no matter how big. Frogs, newts, small lizards, and lizards not so small, even armored giants like the stegosaur.

The ants had been all over one of the slow-witted grazers long before it knew what was happening. With instinctive accuracy, trains of hoplite majors, fierce soldier ants, attacked the creature's eyes, stinging. They crawled into its mouth, tearing at soft tissues. They choked its snuffling nostrils. They opened seams in the skin between its armored scales, biting till the blood flowed, then overrunning the site.

The beast had been driven out of its senses by pain and venom. Its system was stunned by mega-doses of the ants' toxic formic acid. The venom did the real damage. The stegosaur had been ready to collapse when it blundered across the she-rex.

Now the Tyrant was under attack. Enraged, she crashed among the trees, felling whole sections with her thrashings.

Each time she brushed up against a tree, or a vine, waves of hoplites poured from the foliage, onto the dinosaur.

The Tyrant's field of vision was blurred, pitted. Her head whipped from side to side, pain-maddened.

She lusted to do battle with an enemy, throwing the full weight and power of her titan supremacy against a tangible foe of flesh and blood.

The ants were elusive, like smoke. Try to grab hold of them, and there was nothing there.

When she butted her head against some

great tree trunk, pulping the ants against it and felling the tree, more ants would stream out of the tree, replacing those that had been killed.

Now the she-rex's brightly colored hide was dulled with patches of what looked like furry rust. The patchwork was especially thick around her head and shoulders, a copper-red hood and cloak. It was made of ants, a crawling second skin of hoplites.

She had had enough of the unequal combat. She wanted out of the forest. She was more than half-blind.

She crashed through the woods, adding to the masses of ants already on her, and broke into daylight.

The hoplites were there, too, their leading waves having emerged from the forest, onto the plain.

From all directions, they arrowed toward the tyrannosaur. They surrounded her, closing in. They swarmed her monstrous clawed feet, clinging to her pillarlike legs.

Suddenly something tore across the sky, traveling from north to south.

A light—a fireball.

The sky was overcast, hiding the sun, but the fireball shone through it. It was very bright, even to the failing sight of the Tyrant.

It flashed overhead, a spear blade of whooshing light. Its passage lit the scene, casting shadows. The shadows moved as the fireball passed, creating a dizzying whirl.

The fireball vanished below the southern horizon. The light dimmed, shadows fading.

It was gone. A faint afterglow marked its passage.

For an instant the landscape was still, frozen, the life on it motionless. Even the pterosaurs seemed pinned in place in midair.

After a pause, there was a tremendous boom, as if the sky had been ripped apart.

The fireball had been traveling faster than the speed of sound. Now the roar of its passage had caught up to it.

The boom sounded like the crack of doom. Which it was. Literally.

The doom of the Age of Reptiles.

The fireball impacted south of the Gulf of Mexico, in the Yucatàn peninsula. The results of that mighty crash may be seen today, in the form of a system of underground caverns, in one of the biggest holes in the world. That was where the fireball hit.

The visitor even has a name, given it by scientists:

Nemesis, the Deathstar.

It wasn't really a star, no more than shooting stars are made of stellar stuff. It was cosmic dust, a bit of stone and ice, about the size of a small island.

It hit the planet like a hammer striking a gong. Pressure waves spread out from the crash site, opening spidery cracks, hundreds and thousands of miles long, in the earth's surface. One such crack became the Grand Canyon.

Valleys were thrust upward, miles into the air, becoming mountains. Sea bottoms cracked, draining their waters into sunless underground depths. Volcanoes sprang into being, chains of them, venting lava, ash, and smoke.

A sinkhole opened, swallowing the valley whole, river, marshes, plains, forests, dinosaurs—and hoplites—all.

It was a dark day, the first of many. The asteroid crash had pulverized mega-millions of tons of rock, turning it into powder, tossing it hundreds of miles high.

There it stayed, a grimy filter floating in the air, blocking out much of the sunlight that would normally have fallen on Earth. Days were an endless gloomy twilight.

With less sun, Earth grew cooler.

The effects of this planetary chill made themselves felt after a number of million years.

The Age of Reptiles was done.

The dinosaurs were dead, or dying out. They

couldn't adapt to changed climatic conditions. The result: mass extinction.

This cleared the way for the rise of the mammals. Including, ultimately, humans.

Dinosaurs were not the only casualties of the period's mass extinctions. The cooling climate also put an end to the swarm raiding Myrmex hoplite ants.

Almost.

2

SAME GENERAL REGION OF OHIO, SIXTY-FIVE million years later. There were rivers and valleys, but not the same ones as in the days of the dinosaurs.

On a weeknight in early spring, after dark, Donny Pike came to Uncle Pete's Trading Post with a bagful of horror.

It wasn't quite a bagful of horror, not yet. The potential was there, but the horror process had not yet begun.

For now, all it was was an ordinary-seeming brown paper bag, rolled at the top.

In the bag were some jars and stuff. Occasionally they rattled while he drove. The bag sat beside him on the front seat of his car. The car was an old clunker, but it ran.

Donny drove north on a four-lane highway. Between long scenic stretches of Ohio countryside, there were towns.

He was between towns. It would have been

scenic if it hadn't been dark. No matter how scenic, though, it wouldn't have registered with Donny. He wasn't a scenery kind of guy. To him, scenery was something standing in the way of where he had to get to, that's all.

He was in his late teens, a high-school dropout. He had a long thin face, and was wiry.

Ahead, on the right, was Uncle Pete's Trading Post. Donny slowed the car, turning into the gravel parking lot.

The shop was a wooden barnlike structure, its short end fronting the highway. In the center of the lot was a concrete island topped by an electric signpost. The electric sign was dark. This early in the season, Uncle Pete only turned it on during weekend nights, in hopes of drawing the tourist trade. There were a lot of attractions along this stretch of road in Haverlee County, little more than a half hour's drive from the nearest big city. There were fields, streams, rivers, lakes. Picnic sites, camping grounds. Hunting, fishing, boating, and hiking. These were seasonal things, and the season had not yet begun, so Uncle Pete kept the sign dark.

At the base of the sign were some small footlights so people could see the sign when it was dark, and not drive into it by mistake.

Outside lights burned on the front of the store. Inside, some of the lights were dark, but not all. Parked to one side of the front door was a car. Uncle Pete's car, Donny guessed. It was the only car in the lot, besides his own.

He pulled up alongside it, gravel crunching under the wheels. He put the car in park. The engine raced, idling heavily.

He listened carefully, hearing a valve tap.

"Great," he said, disgusted. "Fixing that'll cost plenty."

Headlights glared on the storefront's plate-glass windows. Donny switched them off.

He turned on the car's overhead dome light. He opened the top of the bag, reaching inside.

He pulled out a pint-sized glass jar with a screw-on metal cap. In it was a hunk of some chalky-white stuff, like plaster.

He held it under the light, squinting at it. He put it back in the bag. He took out a baby-food jar. The label had been steamed off. Small holes were punched in the top of the lid.

In the jar was a green leaf, half-folded. Donny shook the jar. A half-dozen ants rattled around inside.

Each ant was about the size of the nail on Donny's pinky. They were pale things, almost transparent, with a light copper tinge.

Donny shook the jar some more, shaking up the ants. He put the jar in the bag.

He killed the engine, switched off the overhead light, picked up the bag, and got out of the car.

The shop stood alone on a lot in a clearing. Where the clearing ended, woods began.

There were no neighbors, no nearby structures. An eighth of a mile north, up the road, was a gas station. Beyond that, behind a ridge, was a town. The ridge hid the town, but the glow of lights showed above it.

A police car passed, going northbound. Instinctively, Donny turned away from it, shoulders hunched, pulling up his jacket collar.

"What've I got to be afraid of? I'm not breaking any laws," he said to himself.

Still, he didn't relax until the police car was out of sight.

For all he knew, maybe he *was* breaking a law. There were so many laws, a guy couldn't turn around without breaking a couple of them, especially if he was trying to make a buck.

Besides, he didn't relish even a routine encounter with the cops. They were sure to find something out of line, and then they would really put the screws to him.

He took out a crumpled pack of cigarettes, flipped one out, and lit up. It was stale, and tasted lousy.

Choking, fighting to keep from coughing, he

went to the store's entrance. It was closed, locked.

He peered through the glass, into the shed-like interior. It was not dark, but dim, with few lights. He didn't see anybody inside.

He started pounding on the door, thumping his fist against the thick safety plate glass.

Someone would come. He'd keep pounding until they did.

This was business.

Inside was the owner-manager, Uncle Pete Shannon, and a store clerk, Annie Pym.

He was "Uncle Pete" for business reasons. He thought it sounded friendlier than just plain "Pete." The name of the store was "Uncle Pete's Trading Post and Souvenir Shop." "Uncle Pete" was a kind of mythical character, embodying the image of a fun-loving favorite uncle with a twinkle in his eye.

Any resemblance between "Uncle Pete" and the real-life, flesh-and-blood boss was purely coincidental.

He was big, heavyset, with a hangdog face. Thin black hair was slicked back as if it had been inked on his head. He was neatly shaved and barbered, always.

He wore a long-sleeve white shirt, dark tie, vest, and pants. The vest and pants came from the same suit.

He wore an old-fashioned accountant's green

eyeshade. It gave his face a green tinge. It made him look like a bland, overgrown lizard.

His eyes were dark, hooded, suspicious.

At one side of the front doors stood a counter, topped by a cash register. Uncle Pete stood behind the counter, checking the day's receipts.

Nearby stood Annie Pym, sweeping up.

She was five feet tall, and weighed less than one hundred pounds. She had dark hair and a thin, pretty face. Her hair was cut in bangs, and fell to her shoulders. Strands of it kept falling across her face. She had a nervous habit of chewing on the ends, in the corners of her mouth. She had wide dark eyes.

She was a junior in high school. Clerking in the store was her after-school job. She worked on weekday afternoons and weekends.

She needed the money. Her family needed the money. Her father was dead. He'd died a couple of years ago, after a long sickness. Her aunt, her mother's sister, was Mrs. Pete Shannon. That's how Annie had gotten the job.

"What the heck? As long as I've got to pay somebody the minimum wage, it might as well be family," Uncle Pete liked to say.

Outside, Donny Pike kept thumping on the door.

Uncle Pete frowned, looking up from his accounts. He eyed Annie, his frown deepening.

"You're supposed to be sweeping, girl, not leaning on that broom," he said.

Annie didn't argue. She had been working on half power. She didn't have a lot of pep. Between school and work, and helping out with the brats at home, she was always tired.

Donny Pike, not tired, kept thumping.

"Can't he see we're closed? Pest! Get rid of him," Uncle Pete said.

Annie leaned the broom against the counter.

"Okay, Pete," she said.

She called him Pete. Everybody did. "Uncle Pete" was strictly fantasyland. The last employee who had made the mistake of calling him Uncle Pete to his face had been fired right on the spot.

Annie went past the end of the counter, turned right, and went to the door. On the other side of the glass stood Donny Pike.

When he saw her, he stopped thumping. He motioned for her to let him in.

She shook her head, mouthing the words, "We're closed."

The store closed at seven P.M., weekdays, as the lettering on the door in front of Donny Pike's face so stated.

"Get Uncle Pete," he shouted. The thick glass door made it hard for him to be heard inside.

Annie shook her head, hands folded over her thin chest.

Donny Pike held up the brown paper bag. "He knows me! Donny Pike! Knows my brother," he said. "I got something for him!"

Annie could just barely make him out. She was cool, watchful. He didn't look like a holdup man, although you never could tell for sure.

On the other hand, he didn't look overly honest, either. That was just a feeling Annie had about him, but her first impressions of people were usually right.

Uncle Pete wasn't the overly honest type. He did business with some pretty strange characters, sometimes. What that business was, Annie didn't know. She minded her own business, but it was impossible not to notice what was going on around her. She guessed that some of Uncle Pete's dealings were on the shady side, but she kept it to herself.

So, maybe the guy did have legitimate business to transact with Uncle Pete. Or not-so-legitimate business. Who cared?

Not she. Let Uncle Pete figure it out.

She motioned for Donny Pike to wait. She went away from the door, out of his view.

"He wants to see you, Pete," she said.

"I told you to get rid of him," Uncle Pete said, not looking up.

"He says you know him."

"Who is he?"

"I don't know. Donny Pike, or something."

"Never heard of him. Get back to your sweeping," he said.

She stood her ground. "He said he had something to sell you."

"So what? This isn't a pawnshop, girl."

The door thumping began again. Evidently, Donny Pike had grown tired of waiting.

"What is he, some kind of a troublemaker?" Uncle Pete said.

"I don't think he's going to go away." Annie had to talk loudly to be heard over the thumping.

"We'll see about that." He hitched up his pants. He came out from behind the counter. Instinctively he reached for his side, where he wore a handgun in a clip-on holster, high on his right hip. The weapon, a neat little .32 pistol, was hidden under his vest. You could see the outline of it, if you knew where to look.

A couple of years ago, long before Annie had come to work for him, he'd shot and killed a holdup man, a famous incident in recent local history. On the surface, it was a clear-cut case of self-defense, a merchant protecting life and property. The dead man had a long criminal record for drunk and disorderly, assault, and petty theft. Uncle Pete was licensed to carry the gun, so there was no beef there. But there were rumors that he and the dead man had been involved in some shady deals, that they'd had a falling-out, and that there was bad blood between them. The idea was that Uncle Pete had lured the other to a meet, promising a make-good, only to ambush and kill him. The police were unable to prove anything more than that he and the deceased had been casually acquainted. Uncle Pete Shannon was a prominent local businessman, while the other was a crook with a record. No charges were filed in the case, and he enjoyed a flurry of HERO MERCHANT SLAYS ROBBER type headlines for a few days, before the buzz died down.

Uncle Pete went to the front door. He didn't recognize Donny Pike, but the other knew who he was.

Pike was babbling something about his brother, about how Pete had done some business with his brother, and so on. It wasn't impossible. Pete Shannon did business with lots of people. All kinds of business, and all kinds of people.

Which didn't mean that he was going to do any with Donny Pike. He'd tell him just that, but not by shouting through a thick glass door.

Uncle Pete looked around, past Donny Pike, making sure that Pike didn't have a few cronies lurking in the background, waiting for him to unlock the door so they could rush him.

He didn't see any. He unlocked the door, the gun on his hip a comforting weight.

He opened the door a few inches, planting the edge of one of his big size-twelve feet against it so it couldn't be forced open.

"Hey, Uncle Pete." Donny Pike grinned, showing a mouthful of bad teeth.

"Can't you read the sign? We're closed."

"I've got some business to do with you."

"Come back when we're open. Ten o'clock tomorrow morning."

"Can't. I'm working then," Donny Pike said.

Pete got ready to close the door.

"Besides, this is private business," Donny Pike said.

Pete looked doubtful, but he didn't shut the door.

"I'm Donny Pike. My brother's Danny Pike. He did some private business with you last year. He sold you a bunch of Indian arrowheads and pots and stuff. He was working on a road crew that found an old Indian burial mound, and he brought the stuff to you . . ."

As he spoke, Donny Pike was watching Pete's face, and noticed when it changed.

"You remember him, Uncle Pete."

"I remember," Pete said, thoughtful.

This part of Ohio had once been home to many Indian tribes, all of them having long ago gone elsewhere, or become extinct. The largely undeveloped countryside was constantly yielding new finds of burial mounds and tombs.

They were of great interest to archaeologists and historians, also to private collectors. And, like most collectors, the ones around here were not too particular about the source of their treasures. There were laws declaring that all such finds were the property of the state, laws that were widely ignored by both buyers and sellers.

Pete Shannon had built up a nice little sideline, buying and selling genuine Indian artifacts. Also semiprecious stones and fossils, which also had their passionate devotees.

Uncle Pete wasn't one of these. Apart from its market value, such stuff was nothing but a bunch of old junk to him. But then, he was a vendor, not a collector.

It was a nice little cash business, tax-free. Which didn't hurt.

Pete recalled Danny Pike, the man and the deal. The man had looked like an older, rougher version of his brother. The find had been a good one, and Pete had profited by it.

"I guess you remember now, huh, Uncle Pete?"

"Pike, right?"

"Donny Pike. Danny's my brother."

"You've got something for me?"

"Yep."

"Okay," Pete said. "Come in."

Donny Pike went inside. Pete locked the door, careful not to turn his back on the other. Pike looked safe, but Pete was cautious.

"Thanks, Uncle Pete. You won't be sorry," Pike said.

"I guess your brother didn't tell you that I don't like being called Uncle Pete."

"No, he didn't."

"Mr. Shannon will do."

"Okay, Mr. Shannon," Pike said, smirking.

The back of Pete Shannon's neck started to get hot.

Pike looked around. It was a kind of five-and-ten store. Most of the items sold for between five and ten dollars.

The long shedlike space was filled with display counters and bins, laid out on a grid of aisles.

Wood was a prominent theme. The building was made out of wood. There were rough-boarded, unpainted wooden plank walls and a wooden floor. There was a large section of wooden furniture: tables with tops made from varnished, polished cross-sectional slices of tree trunks. Chairs and couches made from tree branches. Hollowed tree stumps that were umbrella stands.

The inside of the place smelled like a lumberyard.

There was lots of other stuff, too. Celebrity pinup wall posters. Glass unicorns. Wind chimes. Rubber-bladed spears and tomahawks. Baseball caps. T-shirts. Chef's hats and aprons with gag sayings printed on them. Little porcelain painted figurines of shepherdesses and milkmaids. Stuffed deers' heads, with glass marble eyes, mounted on wall plaques, ready for hanging.

There was some camping and outdoor equipment, not much. Pete couldn't make the kind of profits off it that he could from the souvenirs and novelties.

"Man, you sure got a lot of junk," Donny Pike said, chuckling.

"You buying or selling, kid?"

"Selling."

"You hope. Okay, get to it. I'm a busy man. What've you got?"

Donny Pike didn't like to be talked to like this, not by anybody, but he let it pass. This was business.

He set the paper bag down on the counter. At the far end of it stood Annie, watching intently.

"Hi," he said.

"Hi," Annie said.

"If you don't have enough work to keep you

busy, Annie, I'll find you some," Uncle Pete said.

Annie made herself look busy. Pete wasn't watching her. He was interested in the bag, in what was inside. So was she.

Donny Pike unrolled the top of the bag. Shannon leaned forward.

"What is it? Arrowheads?"

"No, Mr. Shannon."

Pike set a glass jar on the counter. In it was a tennis-ball-sized, yellow-white chunk of stuff. It looked like a bunch of grapes that had shrunk to raisins, then been coated in plaster. The stuff encrusting it was soft, powdery. Flakes of it dusted the inside of the jar.

It wasn't a semiprecious stone, or a Civil War relic, or even an Indian potsherd. It looked like a piece of plaster.

"What is it, dinosaur dung?"

Donny Pike was not so easily baited. He smiled, showing that he took no offense at Pete's slighting comment.

"Funny you should mention that, Mr. Shannon," he said, "because a fellow told me that the place where that was found had been sealed away since the days of the dinosaurs."

"Maybe there's a market for dinosaur dung, kid, but it's out of my line."

Pike shook his head. "Oh no, Mr. Shannon.

That ain't it. The dinosaurs are dead, but what I've got here is alive and kicking."

"That crud in the jar doesn't look too lively to me."

"It will. First, I need a glass of water."

"Why, you thirsty?"

"For the demonstration."

"Look, kid, I don't have time for magic tricks—"

"It's no trick, Mr. Shannon. It's real, and it's like nothing you or anybody else ever saw, I promise you that."

"If this is some kind of practical joke . . ."

"I wouldn't waste your time or mine with jokes," Pike said. "Now, you got a glass of water or not?"

"I'll get it," Annie said.

She turned and walked off, not waiting to see if Uncle Pete approved or not. He must not have disapproved, because he didn't call her back or try to stop her.

She went into the employees' washroom, returning a moment later with a glass of water. She set it down on the counter. There was a film on the glass, but it could be seen through.

Donny Pike reached into his pocket and took out a penknife.

Uncle Pete stepped back, widening the gap between himself and the youth. That way, in case Pike turned out against all logic to be a homicidal maniac, and lunged for him with the knife, Pete would have time to draw his gun and drop him.

Pike opened the knife, unfolding a four-inch blade. He set it down in front of him. He opened the lid of the glass jar, shaking the yellow-white lump out into the palm of his hand.

With the knife, he cut a fingernail-sized piece off the lump. It contained about five or six of the raisinlike globules, all crusted together. A pinch of crumbly powder dusted the countertop.

Pike put the large lump back in the jar, sealing the lid. Holding the fragment between thumb and forefinger, he offered it to Uncle Pete.

"Check it out," he said, dropping it on Pete's palm.

Uncle Pete said, "What am I supposed to do with it?"

"I want you to handle it for yourself so you'll see I'm not trying to scam you," Pike said.

Uncle Pete held the piece under the light. The white crust was yellow with age. It was brittle, like a dried mudball, and lightweight. The globules looked like shrunken berries.

It was striped with faint threadlike lines of green and copper, as was the larger piece from which it had been taken.

"Okay, I've looked at it," Pete said. "Now what?"

"Drop it in the water," Pike told him.

Uncle Pete held it above the glass, hesitating. "It's not going to blow up or anything . . . ?"

"No. It's not one of those chemistry deals, Mr. Shannon. It's something different. Better."

Pete dropped the piece in the water. It broke the surface with a soft plop. It didn't sink straight down, but kind of drifted to the bottom.

"Nothing's happening," he said.

"You got to wait. Takes about five minutes."

"And then what, kid? I mean, what am I supposed to be looking for here? Give me a clue."

"Life."

"Huh? I don't get you."

"Life happens, Mr. Shannon. Them little things in there come alive."

"Sure."

"Wait and see what happens, Mr. Shannon, before you call me a liar."

"Nobody's calling you anything, kid, so don't get your back up. I just want to know the name of the game, that's all."

"You handled that piece of—what'd you call it? Oh, yeah, dinosaur dung."

"I was just joking."

"I'm not. It's dead, right?"

"If it ever lived, which I doubt. It's a mineral of some sort, I'd say."

"You would," Donny Pike muttered, smug. "And you'd be wrong."

"What is it, then?"

Annie said, "Something's happening."

The lump in the water had started to fizz. A very mild fizzing, slow and easy, spreading tiny bubbles throughout the glass.

"That's the outer coating dissolving," Pike said.

On the bottom of the glass sat the small berrylike cluster, shedding its powdery crust, turning it into bubbles.

The water changed color. First, it had a ghostly, greenish-white tinge, the color of the crust.

After a half minute, the color darkened, shading into an equally pale copper hue. A faint hue, the lightest shading of copper.

The globules were taking shape now. They no longer looked like shrunken raisins. They swelled, soaking up water like sponges, plumping up.

Their surfaces were smooth, curved. Swollen to bursting. Each globule was about the size of a medium pearl, only longer and more oval.

Copper pearls.

The crusty paste was what held them together. Once it dissolved, they came apart, scattering a half-dozen units on the bottom of the glass.

Uncle Pete peered at them. "What are those things? They look like seeds. . . ."

"Eggs, Mr. Shannon. They're eggs."

"Eggs?"

Annie stood leaning forward, her folded arms resting on the countertop. Her head rested on her arms as she stared into the glass.

"They're moving," she said.

3

THE COPPER PEARLS—EGGS—*WERE* MOVING.

It wasn't some fluke of the dissolving action. What had dissolved was the dried paste, holding the egg cluster together. Most of the stuff had dissolved, going into solution. A few tiny lumps lay on the bottom of the glass, leaking long thin lines of bubbles that rose to the top of the water.

The copper-colored water.

The fizzing had more or less stopped, but the eggs moved. They squirmed, bending.

They hadn't dissolved. The paste had dissolved. They had grown. They weren't growing anymore.

Now they were twitching.

"Cute," Uncle Pete said, impressed despite himself. "What are they, some kind of Mexican jumping beans or something?"

"Life, Mr. Shannon. They're alive."

Annie said, "So are Mexican jumping beans.

They jump because they've got tiny little insects inside them."

"That so?" Pike said, interested. "Maybe that's not so far off the mark, then."

The eggs were now shaped like grains of rice, but bigger. One end was wider than the other.

They writhed, making horseshoe shapes as they tried unsuccessfully to make both ends meet.

"Is that it? Is that all they do? Because if it is, it's going to have a very limited novelty appeal," Uncle Pete said.

Lines formed lengthwise on the eggs, running from end to end, like curved seams. The smaller ends puckered, wrinkled, and tore.

"They're coming apart," Annie said, fascinated.

Pete eyed the nearest egg, which lay curled along the bottom rim of the glass. Something pale, coppery, and active stuck its tip out of the torn narrow end.

The creature inside was shedding its egg case. It was wormlike, made of ringed segments.

It didn't have a head. Or eyes, features, antennae, or limbs. It was smooth-bodied, except for those ringed segments.

It forced its forward, narrow end out of the egg case, which was more like a semisolid outer skin. The egg case peeled back from the tip, like an exploding cigar.

The larva, or grub, forced its way out of the egg case, shedding it like a second skin.

Soon, six coppery grubs floated in the water, littering the bottom of the glass with the shredded husks of cast-off egg cases.

Shannon said, "Not bad, but where do we go from here?"

"I'll show you," Pike said.

He reached into the bag and took out the baby-food jar, the one with the ants in it. He set it down near the glass.

In the jar was a curled leaf, green, but turning brown at the edges. Ants crawled up and down it.

Copper-colored ants.

They were small, a little larger than the larvae. They were the same color as the larvae. They were in constant motion.

They were new. At the same time they were impossibly old, without a doubt the oldest living things on Earth.

When full-grown, each ant would be as big as a wasp, and more dangerous and mean-tempered. They weren't full-grown. Yet.

Attached to the leaf and stem were a few brown nutlike objects. Copper brown. They were gumdrop-sized and -shaped, flattened at both ends. One end was anchored to the leaf.

Most of the pods were on the sheltered inside of the tube, formed by the curled leaf.

"Ants," Uncle Pete said.

Pike pointed a finger at the larvae. "See those grubs? Take them out of the water, and in a few hours they'll spin these cocoons."

Now, he was pointing at the leaf pods. Actually, they weren't cocoons, they were *pupae,* but the general idea was about the same.

"Then, in about a day or two, those cocoons will hatch out a bunch of ants, like the little guys in this jar," Pike said.

He leaned back, a look of triumph on his face. "Now, is that something, or isn't it?" he said.

Uncle Pete shrugged. "It's okay if you're into ants. Personally, I can take them or leave them. Mostly leave them."

Annie watched the ants, scrambling around inside the jar. "They're kind of cute," she said.

"Let them get into the potato salad at the next picnic, and see how cute they look to you then," Uncle Pete said.

He turned to Donny Pike. "An interesting nature study, but why bring it to me?"

"You're a businessman. You buy and sell things," Pike said.

"I can get all the ants I want myself, just by going out and digging up the nearest anthill."

"Not like these," Pike said, still smiling. "I

don't pretend to be an expert on ants, but I know a little something about the outdoors. I've spent most of my life hunting and fishing these parts, and I've never seen ants like this. Not with that copper color."

"That might be of interest to another ant, but not me."

"And I've never seen or heard of any ant, or any other kind of bug, for that matter, that turns from a dried-up egg to a living, moving thing when you drop it into water. Because there ain't no such thing—except for this," Pike concluded.

"Maybe."

"No maybe about it, Mr. Shannon."

Pike showed the other jar, the one with the dried-up egg cluster in it. "There's not going to be any others. This is the only one of its kind. I know," he said. "The less there is of a thing, the more valuable it is. I know that much about collecting. It's the same for old comic books, or spotted owls, or Indian arrowheads.

"Well, this is the only one of its kind. And they're not making any more of them."

"So you say."

"You ever seen anything like this, Mr. Shannon? A piece of dried-up old crud, and you put it in water, and in a few minutes it becomes a living, moving thing?"

"I'm no expert on bugs," Uncle Pete said.

"You're an expert on novelties. If this isn't a novelty, what is?"

"It might be worth a couple of bucks to the right guy, kid. Not necessarily to me," Uncle Pete said.

"If that's how you feel, Mr. Shannon, I won't take up any more of your time."

Pike started to reach for the jars, to put them away. Uncle Pete motioned for him to stop.

"What's your hurry? As long as you're here, we might as well talk," he said.

"I don't want to put you out. Maybe I ought to try a museum or something. One of those professor fellows might be interested."

"Those professor fellows ask a lot of questions. That's their business. They want to know all about a specimen."

Pike grinned knowingly. "Oh, so now it's a 'specimen,' huh? Looks like we're making progress in the negotiations."

"I might be interested," Uncle Pete admitted. "Purely as a speculative investment of a few dollars. In the interests of science."

"Science, sure. How much?"

"Before we talk money, how about some background on this thing?"

"Okay, Mr. Shannon. I'm a construction worker. I've been working one of those riverfront improvement jobs. Shoring up the levees, dredging the channels, widening the shoreline.

"A week or so ago we were doing some digging and we broke into a cave. It must've been sealed up for a long, long time. Like forever. One of the guys on the crew, who took a college course in geology, said he thought it must've been millions of years old.

"I was in the cave, clearing it out with a pick and shovel. It had to be done that way, because the space was too small to get any heavy machinery into.

"All that was in there was rocks and dirt, except for a patch of this dried, crumbly stuff. It was in the corner, on a high ledge, a heap of it about as big as a flower bed.

"I didn't know what it was. For all I knew, maybe it *was* dinosaur dung. I broke off a piece and stuck it in my pocket, to check out later. That's the piece in the jar.

"It was bigger when I found it. It was in my shirt pocket. There were some puddles down there and I was splashing around in them and got wet. My shirt got partially soaked through.

"Later, when I was in the locker room at quitting time, changing into my street clothes, I found a bunch of grubs crawling around in my pocket," Pike said.

"Ugh." Annie grimaced.

Pike grinned. "That's what I said. I was

grossed out. I dumped them out and squashed them. I turned my shirt pocket inside out to make sure I got them all.

"That's when I found something amazing.

"Like I said, my shirt got only partially soaked through. If it'd got soaked all the way through, the whole piece of egg cluster would probably have turned into grubs, and that'd've been the end of it.

"But only part of the piece turned to grubs and came alive. The rest stayed dry. Except on one side, which had gotten wet, but not wet enough. There, the eggs had plumped up, but they hadn't hatched. I could see them, set in the piece like pebbles in a mudball. I could see the grubs moving around inside the eggs.

"I knew I had something, even if I didn't know what. I would have gone back for more, but it was quitting time, and the site was closed. Anyway, I'd be back working in the hole the next day, where there was plenty more of the stuff for the taking, so what was the rush? That's how I figured.

"When I got home, I tried out some experiments. I broke off pieces from the cluster and put them in water. Sure enough, they turned into grubs, just like you saw."

"Wait a minute," Uncle Pete said. "You said this was a riverside cave. How come the water didn't make all the egg clusters come alive?"

"Glad to see you're paying attention, Mr. Shannon. It was a riverside cave, not a river cave. It was buried in the bank, not under the river.

"And it was airtight. A cave-in sealed it off a long, long time ago. When we first broke into it, you could hear a hiss, like air escaping from a leaky tire.

"When we broke in, a little water got in, not much. Just on the floor. The cluster was on a ledge, high on the cave wall, so it didn't get wet. Not then, anyway. But I'm getting ahead of myself.

"When I tried out those experiments, I found out a few things. You can't keep the grubs in the water for too long. They drown. After a couple of hours they stop swimming and sink to the bottom. You can take them out of the water, but they don't do anything. They just lie there, dead.

"But that takes a couple of hours. Take them out before that, while they're still moving, and they're fine.

"When I had a dozen grubs, I put them in a jar, with some leaves and a handful of grass. I punched some holes in the lid for air. I put the jar on the shelf.

"Next morning, they were still grubs, alive and kicking. Crawling, anyway. Some of the leaves and blades of grass showed signs of being nibbled.

"I went to work. That's where I got a real kick in the head," Pike said.

"On the other hand, that's what makes the egg cluster so rare, and valuable," he added, looking slyly at Pete.

Uncle Pete kept a straight face.

Pike went on. "During the night, one of the walls at the digging site had collapsed. The cave was flooded. The bed of egg clusters was washed away into the river, lost.

"That specimen in the jar is all that's left of it."

"Except for all the grubs that come out of the egg clusters in the river. Once they're in water, they come alive. As we've seen for ourselves," Pete said.

"They're buried under tons of mud at the bottom of the river," Pike said.

Uncle Pete shrugged, outwardly neutral. "Could be."

"Depend on it. You haven't seen anybody else coming up with these little darlings, have you?"

"It's not exactly what I'd call front-page news."

"Not to the average guy, but you're always looking for strange stuff, rare stuff," Pike said.

Uncle Pete nodded, conceding the point.

"Well, I don't have to tell you how I felt when I found out that the cluster had been washed away, gone forever. Pretty bad. That was all there was of it, and there wouldn't be any more.

"When I got home that night, there weren't any more grubs, either. They were all gone. In their place was those brown pods you see.

"Cocoons. I figured that's what they must be. The grubs hadn't got out of the jar. The lid was closed tight. No, the grubs were in the cocoons.

"I decided to keep an eye on them, see what developed. After all, it couldn't do me any harm, and it wasn't costing me anything. Maybe in a few weeks, or a few months, something would hatch out. I was interested in seeing what it would be.

"A day later the ants hatched. I saw some of them come out of the cocoons. They're some strange ants. I never saw any ants like that, like they're made of copper.

"They're not red ants. That's not red. That's a whole different color. It's copper.

"Another funny thing. I had them for a couple of days. They weren't eating. You'd think that they'd eat the same thing as the grubs, but they don't.

"They wouldn't touch the leaves and grass, not a bite. I didn't know what to feed them. What do ants eat? I tried some chopped-up bits of lettuce and pieces of fruit. No dice. They weren't eating, and they were getting weaker. They weren't running around all over the place, like they are now.

"I was getting desperate. I tried meat scraps, sliced real fine. The ants went for it like there was no tomorrow. Wolfed it right up.

"Since then, that's what I've been feeding them, and they've been thriving on it. Whatever they are, they're meat eaters.

"They're one of a kind, in more ways than one," Pike said, finishing up.

Uncle Pete stroked his chin, thoughtful. "Strange story."

"It's true," Pike affirmed. "Heck, you've seen the evidence for yourself with your own eyes.

"So—you interested? Want to deal, or not?"

Uncle Pete looked at Annie. "Go clean the stockroom, girl."

"I already did, Pete."

"Clean it again."

She could take a hint. She turned, crossing toward the stockroom. It was well out of earshot of the counter. Pete had sent her away so she wouldn't hear him talking prices with Donny Pike.

That was how she knew he was going to do the deal and become the new owner of the ants.

4

MAGIC INSTANT ANTS!
Just add water and watch 'em
grow—*grow*—*GROW!!!*

That was the headline on a full-page ad that ran in a number of comic books during their spring issues.

The centerpiece of the ad was an illustration, which took up most of the page. It was a dynamic drawing, in bold colors, of a horde of monstrous ants.

In the middle ground was an anthill, looking as big as a mountain. It was topped by a glittering crystal boxlike structure, resembling a futuristic streamlined glass castle.

In the top was an open hatch. Ants were pouring out of it, a seemingly endless stream. They poured down the hill, into the foreground, threatening to burst out of the borders of the panel, into the reader's lap.

They were drawn in classic comic-book style, each armored ant crackling with energy, dramatically foreshortened, each spiky detail lovingly depicted.

The artist who had been given the assignment had never seen the product. That was just as well, since it kept him from being hampered by any reality inputs.

The artist had gone wild. His ants were the color of the planet Mars. Mars, the god of war. They were a mass of fearsome, armored six-legged killing machines.

Although he didn't know it, the artist had come close to capturing the reality of the mail-order ants.

But that discovery lay in the future. The not-too-distant, nightmare future.

The ad copy, the text, pitched the product. "The Magic Instant Ants," as they were called, were only part of "Ant Castle."

The castle was the fabulous clear plastic cube that the ant colony was housed in, an idealized version of which crowned the anthill in the drawing.

The ad promised that this was the ultimate ant-colony set. There were other self-contained ant-colony sets on the market, yes. But none of them came close to this.

Only Ant Castle came with Magic Instant Ants.

Just add ordinary tap water to the "Egg Cluster" included in the kit, and within minutes, the "Magic Ant Horde" would begin aborning.

In a day, these "Lethal Larvae" would encase themselves in "Cocoons of Doom," quickly hatching out into world-shaking, awesome "Mighty Magic Ants"!

So said the ad. It was in there, selling hard.

For once, the pitchman's fantastic promises would fall far short of the terrifying truth-to-come.

In the meantime, it sold a lot of Ant Castles, nationwide.

Buyers were told to mail their orders to TPP, Inc. That stood for Trading Post Products, Inc.

The address was somewhere in Ohio.

Delivery time was between four to six weeks (once the buyer's check had cleared).

One of those who answered the ad was young Robbie Kellerman, of Twin Oaks, Ohio. The town was about twenty miles north of Uncle Pete's Trading Post.

He was the first to receive an order of Magic Instant Ants.

Also known as Myrmex hoplites.

5

THE ANTS CAME ON A MONDAY.

So did Mrs. Lacey Cunningham.

At first, there was no question as to who was the more dreaded pest. Mrs. Cunningham won, hands down.

But that was early in the game.

It was about three-thirty in the afternoon, in Twin Oaks, on Maple Street. The sun was warm, the sky was blue, and the trees were green. Birds sang, bugs buzzed.

It was a tree-lined street with nice lawns and neat, modest two-story white houses. Modest-sized, not modest-priced. It was a middle- to upper-middle-class neighborhood.

The street was quiet, with little traffic.

When Gwen Kellerman came home from school, she found her kid brother, Robbie, waiting outside the house.

He was in seventh grade, at junior high

school. She was sixteen, a junior in high school.

The junior high was closer to their house than the high school. They both got out at the same time, three o'clock. Robbie should have been home at least ten minutes before Gwen.

He stood on the sidewalk in front of the house, his face unhappy. He had a crew cut and wore glasses. He had a high forehead with a ridge in it, giving him a kind of double dome.

He wasn't a bad-looking kid, even if he was her kid brother, thought Gwen. When he grew out of the awkward age, he might even be kind of cute.

But for now, there was something about his frowning intensity that reminded her of a bug. The more serious he was, the more pinched and buglike he looked.

Now he really looked insectoid.

Gwen had no worry about her looks. She was perfect. Well, almost perfect. There was a tiny bump on the bridge of her nose that she could have lived without, and she'd have liked to be a few pounds thinner.

Apart from that, she was satisfied with her looks. It wasn't as if she had anything to do with it. She was just lucky enough to have been born good-looking, so she might as well enjoy it. Which she did.

She had blond hair, blue eyes, and a trim, athletic figure.

She could have gotten a ride home from any of a number of her friends, male and female, but she had chosen to walk, for the exercise.

Now she was greeted by the sight of her kid brother, moping around with a long face.

She said, "How come you're not inside with your nose buried in a comic book or watching TV?"

"There's good news and there's bad news," he replied. "The good news is that Mom and Dad are gone."

"That *is* good news."

"The bad news is that Mrs. Cunningham is here."

"Already? It's early yet."

"She's already moved in and made herself at home."

Gwen glanced at the house. "You were inside?"

"Naw. I peeked. She's in the kitchen, yakking on the phone."

She remembered not to frown. It caused wrinkles.

Still, she was irked. She shifted her grip on her schoolbooks, cradling them with one arm. She put her other hand on her hip. She glared houseward, ominously tapping her foot, like a cat thumping its tail before it pounces.

"I don't see why Mom and Dad let that woman take over the house for the week they're gone," she said.

Robbie smirked. "Don't you remember what they said? 'It's not that we don't trust you, it's just that we'll feel better knowing there's an adult in the house.' "

His face twisted savagely, mockingly as he imitated the words of their parents.

"I can see why they wouldn't trust you," Gwen said. "But why me?"

"Maybe they met some of your boyfriends," Robbie suggested.

"Very funny. Why don't you go try your wit out on Mrs. Cunningham?"

"I hate her."

Gwen looked doubtful. "That's pretty strong."

"Yeah, like you don't." His tone was mocking.

"I don't."

"Yeah, sure."

"I don't. Hate. The. Woman. I don't," Gwen said. "I don't like her, but I don't hate her."

"That wasn't what you said the last time she was here."

"I don't remember what I said. But I don't hate her. I don't hate anyone," Gwen said loftily.

"You are such a phony." Robbie rolled his eyes. "Wait'll the first time she tells you to do something you don't want to do, or makes noises like a parent."

"In that case, I'll just have to show her the error of her ways."

"I can't wait to see that."

"What are you doing out here anyway, little man?"

"Waiting for you," Robbie said. "I figured I'd go inside at the same time as you. Then, while you're hassling with her, I can slip by her, and not have to relate."

"That devious brain of yours is always working." The tone of her words was not without admiration.

He shrugged. "I can't get by on my looks, like some people."

"Pretty is as pretty does," Gwen said lightly.

"That's a good one. Why don't you try that one out on Mrs. Cunningham?"

"I might," she said.

He fidgeted. "Let's go inside."

"What's the matter? Too much sunshine and fresh air starting to get to you?"

"Yes. It makes me nervous."

"This must be the longest you've been outside all year."

"If you think the outdoors is so great, just try to find a place to plug in a video game."

"The outdoors is going to look pretty good to

you once you're in the same house with Mrs. Cunningham."

"I don't care. My door has a lock."

"Yes. What is it you do, all those hours you're locked by yourself in your room?"

Robbie got red in the face. "Never mind about that!"

"You don't have to shout," Gwen said.

"You're picking on me."

Gwen looked upward, as if calling on heaven to witness how long-suffering she was.

She tsk-tsked. "Get a grip on yourself, little man. We can't afford to fight now. We've got to stick together against Mrs. Cunningham.

"It's us against her, Robbie. *E pluribus unum,* and all that."

"What?" Robbie scowled, eyes small and beady behind thick glasses, veins standing out on the sides of his high forehead.

At that moment he really looked buglike to Gwen. She fought the impulse to swat him, verbally or otherwise.

"E pluribus unum," she repeated patiently, as if to an idiot. The phrase had come up in her social studies class today, and was fresh in her mind.

"It's the motto on U.S. coins," she said. "It's Latin. It means 'united we stand.' "

"No, it doesn't. It means, 'out of many, one.' Shows what you know."

She shrugged. "Same difference."

"No, it's not."

"Suit yourself. Are you happy, now that you've shown off how smart you are?"

"Smarter than you."

Gwen sighed. Exasperated, she looked away, toward the house.

In the corner of a front picture window, inside, a clawlike hand held a pulled-back curtain so a face could peer out.

The face was white, haggard, and clownlike. The way it floated up, from behind the glass pane, it looked ghostly, spectral. The ghost of a dead clown.

For an instant it gave Gwen a bit of a start. A shivery tingle ran down her spine.

The hand let the curtain fall, hiding the face.

It was Mrs. Cunningham, of course.

"Snoop," Gwen muttered, her lip curled.

"What?"

"Not you, little brother. Her. Mrs. Cunningham."

"What about her?"

"She was watching us from the front window just now. Spying on us."

Robbie looked at the window. "She's not there now. But I believe you. She's always sticking her nose in other people's business."

"She's sneaky, too," Gwen said.

She reached a decision.

"I'm going to show you how mature I can be, Robbie. I'm willing to let bygones be bygones, and call a truce between us, at least until Mrs. Cunningham is gone."

"It's a deal," he said, sticking out a hand. "Shake."

They shook hands.

"E pluribus unum," Gwen said.

"Which means, get her before she gets us."

"That's a little drastic, don't you think?"

"Wait until you've been around her for a while, Gwen."

"Well"—she sighed—"we've stood around here long enough. Let's go in and say hello to the old monster."

"I'd rather say good-bye to her," Robbie said.

They went into the house.

They didn't know anything about monsters yet, real monsters, but they would.

6

THE HOUSE WAS HOT AND SMELLED OF HEAVILY spiced meat being cooked. It hit Gwen and Robbie with an almost physical impact as soon as they came through the side door into the kitchen.

They made faces at each other.

Mrs. Cunningham was cooking. She was in the middle of things. The counters were covered with pots and pans. It looked as though half the spice rack had been raided to season the roast that was now baking in the oven.

The heat brought color and a fine sheen of sweat to Gwen's face. She could hear the fatty meat sizzling and bubbling in its own juices. All the windows were closed; there was no air. She felt slightly ill.

In the middle of it all was Mrs. Cunningham.

Mrs. Cunningham was a neighbor, a widowed lady who lived here on Maple Street, a few houses away. She was a friend of Gwen and Robbie's parents. Not a close friend, exactly, but she was useful. When the Kellermans went away on vacations, Mrs. Cunningham would kind of keep an eye on the place.

That was in her line, because she was a snoopy kind of a character anyway, who was always keeping tabs on her neighbors, and on the comings and goings on the block.

A couple of times, when Gwen and Robbie's parents had gone away on short trips, they had arranged for Mrs. Cunningham to stay over at their house and mind the kids.

That suited her fine, since the Kellermans had a well-stocked refrigerator and a big color TV.

It suited Gwen and Robbie less well.

They marched into the kitchen, grim-faced.

Mrs. Cunningham had dyed orange hair, of a color not found in nature. Beneath the stiff, sprayed, unnatural coif, her face was old and wrinkled, heavily made up. She had watchful, baggy brown eyes, and a long space between her nose and upper lip, like an orangutan. Her thin lips were heavily smeared with red lipstick, a clown's mouth.

She wore a flower print dress, an apron, and thick-soled orthopedic support shoes. She smelled of a sickly-sweet thick violet scent, mixed with the medicinal smell of muscle-relaxing liniment.

Gwen nodded to her, grudgingly recognizing her existence. "Hello," she said coolly.

Robbie didn't say anything. He bobbed his head in her direction as he hurried out of the kitchen, into the hall. Gwen followed.

"Hello, children! Where are you going?" Mrs. Cunningham asked.

"Out," Gwen replied, over her shoulder. "I have to change first."

Robbie didn't say anything. He dashed up the stairs and into his room, slamming the door.

Gwen went upstairs, not running, but not dawdling, either. She left Mrs. Cunningham standing in the hall below, looking up the stairwell, hands on hips.

"My, my. We're in a hurry today," she said.

Ignoring her, Gwen crossed the landing to her room.

"We'll talk later," Mrs. Cunningham called after her.

Gwen entered her room, firmly closing the door behind her and locking it. The room was bright, clean, airy, and normally smelled sweet and fresh, like Gwen herself.

Now, though, there was a faint but unmistakable smell of violets and liniment.

Gwen's nostrils wrinkled. Mrs. Cunningham had been in her room recently.

Gwen frowned darkly, eyes flashing. She looked around for signs that her belongings had been handled, her privacy further invaded.

Was the jewelry box on her dresser in exactly the same place she had left it before leaving for school this morning, or had it been moved a few inches?

She had a habit of not quite closing the dresser drawers all the way, but leaving them a fraction of an inch open. They were all closed tight now.

On her desk, a bundle of letters that she kept in a holder were arranged a little more neatly than they had been. Not that there was anything compromising in the letters. If there had been, she wouldn't have left them out in the open.

There were things of hers that were private and confidential, for her eyes only. They were well hidden, where they wouldn't be found by a curious mom, snoopy kid brother, or nosy busybody like Mrs. Cunningham.

That wasn't the point. This was her room, and her stuff, and not to be messed with. Period.

She did a slow burn. She bit down on the inside corners of her lips, her mouth a straight line.

The windows were open, about six inches. She flung them open wide, letting in the fresh air.

She took off her blouse and skirt. The skirt was clean and could be worn again. She hung it up in her closet. The blouse could use a washing, so she set it aside, to toss in the hamper.

She thought twice about it. While she was staying over, Mrs. Cunningham would be doing the wash. Gwen didn't want her pawing her clothes. She made a mental note to wash it herself.

She pulled on a pink-and-white T-shirt and a pair of soft, well-worn, sky-blue jeans. She slipped into a pair of loafers.

She ran an oversized shocking-pink plastic comb through her long blond hair, glinting with bronze highlights.

Studying herself in the mirror, she gave her head an artful little toss so the hair would fall just so.

She was ready to go out.

"And not a moment too soon," she said to herself.

It was warm now, but it might get cooler later. She grabbed a light denim jacket from the closet, tossing it over her arm.

She paused at the door, hand on the doorknob, looking back. She tried to fix the location of everything in her mind so she'd know if her stuff had been messed with while she was out.

She went out, into the hall, nearly colliding with Mrs. Cunningham.

"Oh!" Mrs. Cunningham said, startled.

Gwen looked her in the eyes, cool and direct. "My room is private, Mrs. Cunningham. I don't like people going into it without my permission."

The older woman was unflustered. "Why, I was just looking to see if anything needed cleaning, dear."

"I'll clean it myself, thanks."

"Of course, dear," Mrs. Cunningham said, simpering. "I hope you don't think I was prying, Gwen."

"Why would I think that? Just because you were in my room when I wasn't around?"

"Why, I wouldn't dream of invading your privacy. Not that a youngster like you has anything to hide, I'm sure."

Her mocking expression suggested that she thought the opposite.

Smiling sweetly, looking the housekeeper in the face, Gwen eased her door shut, closing it so that it fell into place with a loud click.

"Maybe I should put up a 'Do Not Disturb' sign," she said.

She eased past Mrs. Cunningham and went down the hall to the landing. From behind the closed door of her brother's room came the sound of synthesized *wheep-bleeps,* booms, and blasts. Robbie was playing one of his video games.

Seeing Gwen's jacket, Mrs. Cunningham said, "Going somewhere, Gwen?"

Gwen went down the stairs. "Yes."

Mrs. Cunningham followed. "Where?"

"I'm going to my friends' house to study."

"That's nice. What friends are those?"

There was no point in not answering, or in telling Mrs. Cunningham to mind her own business. She was capable of going through the phone book and calling as many friends and neighbors as it took to find Gwen—and had done so in the past.

Besides, she would just quiz Robbie about her whereabouts, and he would tell her the truth just to make her go away and stop bothering him.

"I'll be with the twins, Ellen and Helen Trent. You know them," Gwen said.

"Yes," Mrs. Cunningham said, sniffing. Her tone said she didn't think much of them, either. "How can you study, when you don't have any books, Gwen?"

"I'm going to the library first."

"Oh. That's nice."

In the front hall, a wall clock said the time was a few minutes before four.

Mrs. Cunningham said, "Dinner's at six."

"That's nice. Too bad I won't be here," Gwen said.

"But I'm cooking a roast, a nice lovely meal for the three of us—you, me, and Robbie!"

"I don't eat meat, Mrs. Cunningham. I'm a vegetarian."

"What?!" Mrs. Cunningham was scandalized, as if Gwen had admitted to something infamous.

Sensing the other was off balance, Gwen pressed the point. "Killing animals and eating them is immoral, Mrs. Cunningham."

"B-but what about my roast? I've been cooking it all afternoon. . . ."

"I'm sorry, but you could've saved yourself the trouble if you'd asked me first. Anyway, you and Robbie can eat it.

"Enjoy," she finished.

Mrs. Cunningham's eyes narrowed. "Your parents didn't tell me anything about your being a vegetarian."

"I'm sure it slipped their minds, what with so much else to think of, like Daddy's big job interview in New York City, and getting ready for the trip."

"I suppose," Mrs. Cunningham said doubtfully.

"In fact, you won't have to cook any meals for me, Mrs. Cunningham. I'll make my own. That's what I do now, anyway. Special vegetarian diet, you know."

"I'll make some vegetables with dinner—"

"Good. That's a lot healthier for you than all that meat. Don't make any for me."

"Why not?"

"I have to have them cooked a certain way. Otherwise, you lose all the vitamins. Besides, I'm not going to be here tonight for dinner."

"Don't be silly! You can't skip a meal."

"I'll get something at a bar," Gwen said.

"A bar?!" Mrs. Cunningham looked like she was choking on something. Her eyes bulged and her face got red. "You listen to me, Gwen Kellerman! You're underage, and it's illegal for you to go into a bar—"

"A salad bar, Mrs. Cunningham."

Mrs. Cunningham fell silent, her mouth open. "Oh," she said.

"What did you think I meant?" Gwen said innocently.

Outside, there was the sound of a motor vehicle rumbling to a halt in front of the house.

"That's my ride," Gwen said, reaching for the door. "Thank God," she added, under her breath.

Only it wasn't her ride at all. It was a brown

delivery van, bearing the logo of a private parcel-delivery service.

Gwen stood in the doorway, hand on the open door, pouting. Behind her, Mrs. Cunningham craned, trying to see what was happening.

The driver's cab door opened, and a brown-uniformed deliveryman got out, package under his arm. He started up the walk, toward the house.

"Why, he's coming here!" Mrs. Cunningham said.

Gwen was mildly interested. Maybe the package was for her. She wasn't expecting anything, but maybe someone had sent her a surprise gift. It wasn't her birthday or a holiday. Maybe it was from a secret admirer.

"I wonder who that could be for," Mrs. Cunningham said, echoing Gwen's thoughts.

The deliveryman was a good-looking guy in his middle twenties.

When he saw Gwen standing in the doorway, he brightened, putting a spring into his steps.

He started to give her a big smile, then he saw Mrs. Cunningham standing behind her. He straightened his face, trying to look serious, businesslike.

Gwen stood with her hands behind her, holding the doorknob. She smiled, turning on the wattage.

"Hi," she said. "Is that package for me?"

"Not unless your name is Robert Kellerman," he said, glancing at the name on the mailing label.

"All right!"

The shout came from the top of the stairs, where Robbie stood looking down at the deliveryman at the front door.

Sneakered feet pounded as he raced downstairs, across the hall, nearly bowling over Mrs. Cunningham.

"Be careful, dear!" she said sharply.

Robbie signed for the package, and the deliveryman got into his van and drove away. Gwen had been vaguely bored ever since learning that the package was not for her.

The package was shoebox-sized and -shaped, wrapped in brown paper, stamped with labels and stickers.

"Cool," Robbie said. "I've been waiting for this for weeks!"

"What is it?" Mrs. Cunningham asked, interested but vaguely suspicious.

"Magic Instant Ants!" Robbie said. He tore off the wrappings, exposing a brightly colored box beneath.

Mrs. Cunningham frowned, disliking the gaudy box, with its bold, oversized ant images. "What is that, some kind of toy?" she said.

"It's not a toy, it's real Magic Instant Ants."

"There's no such thing as magic, Robbie."

"No kidding."

Noise in the distance neared, turned onto Maple Street, and rolled up in front of the house.

The sound was part machine, part music. The machine was a red muscle car with a lot of engine under the hood. The windows were open. The car's sound system was blasting music.

Stopped, the car looked like it was poised on tiptoes, ready to take off running. Even idling, the big engine made the car shake. In the rear, shiny tailpipes trembled.

In the car were two guys and Ellen and Helen, the twins.

Gwen waved. The car horn honked and its occupants waved back.

Mrs. Cunningham shuddered. "That dreadful noise! Robbie, what are you doing?"

She was torn between being annoyed by the music and keeping an eye on Robbie and his new toy.

He had the box open, lifting the lid on a clear plastic-bagged bundle containing clear plastic squares and rods, bags of dirt, and other things.

His eyes were bright, shining with a fixed intensity.

Mrs. Cunningham distrusted that look. It

promised mischief. And the scientific-insectoid look of the packaged ants was alarming.

"Bye," Gwen said.

"Gwen, where are you going?"

"To the library, with the twins, like I said." She nodded toward the girls in the car.

"But who are those boys?"

"The McBane brothers, Duncan and Gordy. They're giving us a ride."

Mrs. Cunningham's lips tightened in prim disapproval. "I'm not sure I approve of that. I don't think your parents would, either."

"What? Riding in a car with some guys? What are you, like, from the Stone Age?"

"A girl has to be careful who she associates with. A nice girl, that is."

"You don't expect me to walk, do you? Get real."

The horn honked again, impatient.

"I've got to go. Good-bye," Gwen said.

"You'll be at the Trent girls' house?"

"Later, yes. Good-bye!" Gwen started forward.

Mrs. Cunningham called after her. "It's a school night, Gwen, so be back by ten o'clock! That's what your parents said."

There was a tone of guess-I-told-*you* in her voice.

"Yes, yes," Gwen said.

"No later!"

Gwen hurried toward the car, Mrs. Cunningham's words following her. Gwen looked back over her shoulder, relieved that it was only the words following her and not Mrs. Cunningham herself.

She hadn't been sure that the woman wouldn't tag along on her heels, getting a good look at the McBane brothers and possibly even firing a few nosy questions about their family background at them.

The car's back door sliced open for her, revealing the interior. Gwen jumped into the backseat, already occupied by Ellen and Gordy.

In the front was Helen and the driver, Dunc.

Gwen shut the door. Mrs. Cunningham stood on the front walk, a few paces from the house. She stared at the car, hands on hips.

"Go," Gwen said. "Go!"

Dunc stepped on the gas. Tires squealed as the car leaped forward, zooming away.

In the rear window, the house and an irate Mrs. Cunningham dwindled and were left behind.

Gwen sank back into the seat, letting out a long breath that she hadn't even realized she'd been holding.

Ellen said, "Who was that funny-looking old woman, Gwen?"

"Mrs. Cunningham. She's staying at the

house, keeping an eye on me and my brother while our folks are away."

"That's good," Gordy said.

"What's good about it?" Gwen demanded.

"I was afraid she was your mother!"

"Shame on you for even thinking it. How can you say that? We don't look anything alike!"

"Yeah, Gordy, what are you, blind?" Dunc said, over his shoulder.

Next to him, Helen turned around in her seat so she could talk to those in the back. "I guess that means we won't be having any wild parties at your house, Gwen," she said.

"You guess right."

"We'll have to have them at our house," Gordy offered.

Ellen said, "Your folks didn't go away, Gordy."

"Then we'll just have to lock 'em in the closet."

Gwen said, "It takes someone like Mrs. Cunningham to make me appreciate Mom and Dad."

"We'll come over to your house and lock her in the closet," Gordy offered.

"Make it soon."

Dunc asked, "Hey, where to?"

"Let's go somewhere to eat. I'm starved," Gwen said. "I could really go for a cheeseburger."

7

"YOU'RE NOT BRINGING ANTS INTO THE house, are you, Robbie?"

"It's my house, Mrs. Cunningham. If I want to bring ants into it, I can."

"I think your parents might have something to say about that. And, since they left me in charge while they're away, I've got a right, a duty, to make sure that they don't come home and find the place overrun by insect pests."

Mrs. Cunningham was dogging him, following him from room to room, trying to get a better eyeball on the suspect package.

In the front hall, Robbie stopped, took the clear plastic bagful of Ant Castle stuff out of the box, and held it up in both hands so Mrs. Cunningham could get a good look at it.

"There's no ants in it, Mrs. Cunningham. See?"

She looked, looked hard. Her lead-colored, slightly pop eyes stared down her nose at the bag, intent. Her gaze fastened on a vial of copper-colored pellets. They were eggs, although she didn't know it.

What she was really looking for was signs of movement, of active insects already on the prowl. She was ready to make a big fuss about that. When she didn't see any, it took most of the wind out of her sails.

Robbie had learned that it often paid to be open and cooperative with adults, since they were usually so clueless that they really didn't understand what he was telling them, anyway.

"See? No ants, Mrs. Cunningham. It's a toy. Okay?"

Not waiting for an answer, Robbie went upstairs. Mrs. Cunningham watched him go. She fretted, temporarily stymied. She had a feeling that the package would lead to no good, but there was a limit as to how much she could interfere with Robbie's everyday routine.

She went into the kitchen, to tend the roasting meat.

"Just the same, I'll keep my eye on that ant material," she said to herself.

In his room, behind a locked door, Robbie got into his Magic Instant Ants.

There was a bed, a night table with a lamp on it, a writing desk, a chair, and a personal computer. A bookshelf was mostly filled with science-fiction and horror paperbacks. The rest of the space was filled with detailed action figures from Japanese monster and technobot movies.

There were lots of stacks of monster and computer magazines, and comic books. A wall was covered with superhero posters and star maps.

Robbie sat on the floor, setting up the Ant Castle.

There was a little instruction pamphlet, but Robbie didn't need it. It was easy enough to figure out. You set up the Ant Castle, filled it with dirt, and activated the Magic Instant Ants.

Easy.

The clear plastic squares and framework rods snapped together, thanks to prefitted tabs and slots. They formed a cube, measuring eight inches on a side. There was a brown plastic base. There was a lid with a sliding hatch.

Inside, two clear horizontal plastic squares served as floors, dividing the space into three levels. In them were square holes, open hatchways.

Robbie put together the clear plastic cube. He was a little disappointed. From the ad, he'd thought it would be a lot bigger. And it was just a simple, basic, square-sided cube, without the futuristic towers and battlements shown in the ad art.

On the other hand, the Magic Instant Ants would be super-cool. Providing they worked, and the whole thing wasn't a gyp.

"It has to work," he said fiercely. "They wouldn't let them advertise it in a comic book if it wasn't true!

"It's not like TV, where you know all the commercials are lies."

Still, an ad in a comic book was a kind of a commercial, even—maybe especially—if it had great art.

He put all such worrisome thoughts out of his mind. After all, if it was a rip-off, they wouldn't have gone to the trouble of making a whole Ant Castle and putting in the kit.

"The Awesome Eggs are cool," he said.

The eggs came in a plastic vial, about the size of an aspirin bottle, with a snap-top lid. A label on the top identified them as AWESOME INSTANT ANT EGGS.

He held the vial up to the sunlight that was streaming through his bedroom window, falling in a square on the floor.

The eggs were heavier than they looked. The vial felt as heavy as if it had been filled with pebbles.

Robbie shook it, producing a pleasant rattling sound.

He popped the top, shaking a few eggs into his palm. They were smooth, shiny, like copper-colored beads. But they had a certain gritty texture, which marked them as somehow organic.

There was something mysterious, compelling about them. Now they were dormant, like seeds. Add water, and they would become life.

If the ad was true.

As he handled the eggs, some of his natural fingerprint oils smeared on them, filming their shells.

As he watched, the smears vanished, as if the eggs had soaked them up.

"Now, that's cool," Robbie said.

Robbie stuck his head into the hallway. He could hear Mrs. Cunningham downstairs, talking on the phone.

He went into the hall, to the landing. He stood with his hands on top of the balustrade railing, looking down.

Mrs. Cunningham was in the kitchen. He couldn't see her, but occasionally he could see her shadow, framed in a rectangle of light that shone out of the kitchen.

He could hear her moving around, from sink to stove, from countertop to table. There was a rattling of pots, and a ringing of glasses, between the drone of her breathless, near-nonstop phone chattering.

Robbie liked to know where she was, at any given time. It was good for his peace of mind.

He went into the bathroom. On the wall, over the sink, was a paper-cup dispenser. It was a long vertical tube, bolted to one side of the mirror.

There wasn't a communal family drinking glass in the bathroom. Dad didn't believe in them, said they spread germs. In many ways, he was a fussy little guy.

So, instead of a glass, there were paper cups. Robbie filled one with water and took it back to his room.

There was a clear plastic tray about the size of a cigarette pack. It was open on the top.

Following the instructions, he put the copper eggs, all of them, into the tray. They plopped into place, rattling like dried beans.

He poured water into the tray, filling it almost to the brim. The copper eggs were completely immersed.

He watched them closely, hoping for some dramatic change.

Nothing happened. After a minute he put them aside, ready for the next step.

The tray was supposed to go in the bottom of the cube. Robbie had to take out the two inner levels. Luckily, they came out without too much trouble.

He decided that before doing anything else,

he would first take a closer look at the instructions.

They listed the proper way to proceed. He followed them.

The kit had come complete with its own bag of soil. It was tan and sandy. Robbie poured the required two inches of soil into the bottom of the cube.

He put the tray of water-soaked eggs in the middle of the cube floor. He fitted in the two level dividers. He snapped on the lid, making sure the hatch was closed.

The rest of the soil would go in later, after the hatching of the Lethal Larvae. Robbie rolled up the bag, wrapping it in a rubber band, before putting it back in the box.

He needed a place to put the cube. He cleared a space at his desk, under a window. The window let brightness into the room, lighting up the whole area.

Robbie set the Ant Castle in the light. The sunlight made the clear plastic cube seem to be made of crystal.

He leaned forward, at eye level with the cube, looking in.

Had the water level in the tray gone down slightly? He wasn't sure, but he thought that it had.

The eggs looked rounder, more swollen.

Their shells had pores, like skin. The pores were the size of pinholes.

On the surface of the water was a thin, oily sheen, shimmering with faint rainbow swirls, like the skin of a soap bubble.

Things were happening.

"Cool," Robbie said. "Maybe this'll turn out to not be bogus, after all."

8

UNCLE PETE'S TRADING POST WAS NOW ANT Central.

One of the back rooms had been turned into an ant factory. The room was long and narrow. A worktable ran along one of the long walls. On the sides were stacked boxes of different sizes and shapes. In them were the makings of the Ant Castle kits. There were boxes of clear plastic squares, boxes of snap-on rods, boxes of plastic bags, even boxes full of boxes.

Heaped in a corner were fifty-pound bags of sandy soil, from a plant supply store. Pete bagged all his dirt. He saved money that way.

He did almost all of the work involved in making and selling Ant Castles. That was because he didn't trust anyone else with the job.

He was afraid they would steal the secret, and end his monopoly on Magic Instant Ants.

He was a man with a secret, a trade secret.

Apart from himself, only Donny Pike and Annie Pym knew the truth.

The secret was the thing itself: the Magic Instant Ants.

That time months ago, when he had first seen the ants, he'd grasped their possibilities as a marketing gimmick.

He'd done some quick boning up on ants, finding out what he needed to know. He was surprised to find out they were pretty complex creatures. You wouldn't think it to look at them, but then, they were so small that you wouldn't think to notice them much at all, until they made pests of themselves, by raiding the kitchen, for instance. Then you would just get rid of them.

The basic proposition, as far as he was concerned, was that they were egg layers. Each colony had a queen. She laid the eggs. They hatched, growing up into workers. Scattered among their numbers were a handful of potential future queens.

There was more to it than that, but that was at the heart of it. Somewhere in the egg cluster that he'd bought from Pike, there had to be a potential queen ant.

Otherwise, he was out of business before he began. If there was no queen, then the ants who hatched from the egg cluster would be the last of their line. When they were dead, that would be the end of them.

And he'd be out the money he'd paid to Pike.

Pete had cultivated the eggs, growing them. He placed the larvae in glass ant nests, which he'd bought from a nature supply store.

The larvae ate, grew, encased themselves in pupae, and in a few days, hatched into copper-colored ants.

Small ones.

They were pygmy versions of their hoplite forebears, the wasp-sized swarm raiders who had been the terror of the dinosaur age.

There was a reason for that. Eons of time had sapped some of the vigor from the eggs. They had been laid down sixty-five million years before, buried in a cave-in during an earthquake.

The eggs had become semipetrified. Not fully petrified, turned to stone. Only the outer shell had become encrusted. Within, the machineries of life were stilled, but not dead. The eggs came from a savage, elemental age, when life itself was young, and the life in them was strong and burning.

It slept, that life, waiting for the touch that would awaken it: water.

The DNA in the eggs was coded to respond when they were soaked in water. In the life cycle of the ants, that had a purpose. The spring rains would cause the eggs to hatch, when there were plants and microlife in abundance for the larvae to feed on. They would not hatch in winter or times of drought.

The eggs had to wait sixty-five million years for the water to come. When it did, the life process cranked into gear, creakily at first, but still powerful enough to bring the larvae forth into the modern era.

They were back, and Pete Shannon had them. He was lucky. He didn't know what he had. The egg cluster was stale, and the first brood hatched from them was puny and undersized. Stunted.

That held for the second generation as well.

The hatchlings had brought forth three potential queens. Pete separated them before they could do battle. Otherwise, they would have fought until all but one was dead, and that one would be the queen.

He had three queens, each in its own glass nest.

The glass nests were tall, thin, and mounted on stands on the worktable. Each was filled with dirt, which the ants had honeycombed with tunnels.

In the base of the nest was the queen's chamber. She was about ten times bigger than the other ants. She was an egg-laying machine, tended by worker ants. They fed her. She laid eggs.

Pete fed the ants chopped-up meat scraps. He had tried other things, but meat was what the ants liked best. At feeding time, he'd open the top of the nests and pour in the meat scraps. The ants would rush up through the tunnels, forage the scraps, and carry them down into the depths of the nest.

He noticed that the foragers never ate any of the scraps when they first got hold of them, but always brought them down intact and untouched, to be redistributed to the ants below.

"Suckers," Pete said.

Once the queens started laying eggs, and those eggs proved viable, the business practically ran itself.

Pete ordered the clear plastic cubes from a novelty-supply-store wholesaler. He paid a local artist, a kid who drew designs for T-shirts and custom car detailing, to design the kit graphics and the ad art.

Whenever one of the queen's chambers was near to full with eggs, he would open a hatch in the base of the stand, scoop out the eggs, and ready them for mailing in the kits.

That kept down the population of the ant nests to manageable proportions. Meanwhile, the queens kept laying more eggs.

The process moved right along.

The ads got a decent response, and Pete found himself doing a nice little mail-order business in Ant Castles, as he called the final product.

He kept a low profile, using post office boxes and other devices to hide his ownership of the ants.

People were funny about bugs. They might have ants in their own houses, but if they should learn that Pete Shannon was running a little ant factory in the back of the store, the next thing you know, they'd stop shopping at the Trading Post altogether, for fear that they'd "get ants" from something they'd bought.

He didn't sell any Ant Castles in his store. Of the others who knew about the ants, Donny Pike had taken his money and gone away, never to return.

As for Annie, he'd grudgingly had to give her a small raise, to keep her mouth shut about the ants.

Now, it was about six P.M. Six P.M., but not six o'clock at night. It was June. The days were getting longer. There was plenty of daylight left at six o'clock.

In another three weeks or so, it would be time to keep the store open weeknights until nine P.M. School would be out, and families would be on the road, taking their vacations.

It would mean longer hours and more work. Pete was already overworked. He was running the store, plus single-handedly running the mail-order ant business.

He was making more money, too. That was important.

The time to cash in on Ant Castles was now. Once the product was out there, it was only a matter of time before some bigger, better-financed company moved into the business.

After all, once they had their own set, they could separate the queen from it and begin producing Magic Instant Acts of their own.

Tending the ant nests was a pain. And there was another downside. Dealing with bugs was tricky. There might be some federal laws against interstate trafficking in ants that he'd broken. True, he shipped only the eggs, and not the actual insects, so that might be a loophole to get him off the hook, if he ever got in wrong with the law.

He moved around the ant room, finishing up the day's chores. There was plenty of light to see by. The back rooms were partitioned off, made of walls but no ceilings. The store's roof had a skylight in it, helping to light the barn-like space.

The sun was still high in the sky, and there was plenty of light coming through the skylight, shining down into the back rooms.

The ants seemed to like it. Anyway, they were sure stirred up, scrambling around inside the tunnels of their glass-walled nests.

The nests of the three queens were like three standing mirrors on a vanity table. Sunbeams struck their sides, silvering them.

The door to the ant room was bolted from the inside. Pete didn't want anybody walking in on him. Outside, there was a padlock, so he could secure the room when he quit it.

He turned on the electric lights, the better to see what he was doing.

In his hand was a collecting jar. His last ant-room chore, before knocking off, would be to collect the latest batch of eggs.

He was collecting them more and more frequently. At first, it had taken a few days for the chambers to fill with eggs. Then it had become a daily event.

In the last ten days or so, he'd had to collect the eggs twice a day. When the chambers became overful with eggs, the workers would move them to other parts of the nest.

That was a problem. The nests were rigged so it was easy to harvest the eggs from the queen's chamber, but hard to reach them anywhere else.

When they were taken through tunnels to other chambers, higher up, it wasn't worth the trouble to retrieve them. Pete let them be.

These eggs would hatch, slowly increasing the numbers in the nest.

The nests were getting overcrowded. Any day now he'd have to thin them out.

For now, though, it was time to harvest the eggs.

He began with the glass nest on the left side of the bench top.

A simple mechanism made collections easy. The queen's egg chamber was at the bottom of the nest. Its floor was built over a funnel-shaped hopper, with a sliding top.

Normally, the top was open. The queen laid eggs, which rolled to the bottom of the funnel. When the funnel was full, the sliding top would be closed, sealing the queen in the chamber so she was safely out of the way.

Then Pete would open a vertical gate in the hopper, emptying the eggs down a slide into the collecting jar.

For the last few days the eggs had been bigger than usual. Some of the biggest of the new batches were almost double the standard-sized eggs. Their pitted surfaces were coarser, more gross.

Pete had separated this new breed. He had high hopes for them, that they would produce larger queens, with greater egg-laying capacity at speedier rates.

He bent to empty the first hopper, eagerly

looking to see how many of the new, larger eggs had been laid.

He blinked, then stared.

"What the—?!"

The hopper was almost empty. Only a few eggs lay at the bottom of the funnel.

Pete's face got red. Veins bulged in his neck. Instinctively, he turned, staring toward the closed door.

His first thought was that he'd been robbed.

That meant Annie, since she was the only other person working in the store, where she'd been since arriving after school.

But no, how could that be? When he wasn't in the ant room, the door was kept locked—padlocked—and he had the only key.

The partition walls were high, and he couldn't picture Annie scaling them. And besides, when could she have done it? He'd been out on the main floor all the time she'd been here, and he'd easily have seen her going over the wall.

No, she hadn't done it. He was sure of that. The girl was too smart to do something for which she'd be the only logical suspect. She might be a thief—Pete suspected everybody of being as crooked as he knew himself to be—but she wasn't dumb.

She hadn't stolen them. But the eggs were gone. He knew, because he'd seen them when he'd come in earlier, during lunchtime. The hopper had been full almost to overflowing with eggs.

So—where were they?

He stood frozen in place, facing the glass nest, leaning forward over the worktable. He was at eye level with the queen's chamber, staring but not seeing.

Movement, assured and purposeful, caught his eye, and he took a closer look.

Two copper-colored worker ants had dropped into the hopper. Others stood above them, on the floor of the chamber, leaning over the edges of the opening.

As Pete watched—and he was now watching—the ants in the hopper picked up one of the eggs and handed it to the ants poised above them.

The egg was standard-sized. All the eggs that still remained in the hopper were standard-sized. That was about two thirds the size of a worker ant.

The ants handled it with ease and assurance, hoisting it out of the hopper and into the waiting mandibles of the ants who were poised to receive it.

One of them wrestled the egg onto her back.

"Her" back. Almost all the ants in the colony, from the queen on down, were female. There were a few lone males scattered throughout the nest. They did no work, and they were largely ignored by the other ants. They existed for a purpose, and they were being saved for a purpose, but their time had not yet arrived.

Of these and other intricacies of the ant social life, Pete Shannon knew nothing, and cared less.

But he was amazed to see the ants carrying away his egg.

The ant with the egg on her back scooted up a long, wormlike tunnel. A second ant tagged along, moving alongside the first, helping to keep the egg securely in place.

They climbed about a third of the way up into the nest. The glass nest was a vertical structure, like a windowpane onto a thin cross section of chambers and tunnels.

They entered a chamber lined with eggs, and added their burden to the pile. Some of the chamber eggs had already hatched, including some of the newer, larger macro-eggs.

They had hatched larvae, some of which seemed as large as caterpillars.

"Or . . . ugh!—maggots," Pete said, gulping.

They were smooth, wriggling, and copper-colored. But this copper hue was deeper, darker, angrier than it had been before.

Anchored to the chamber walls and floor, even its roof, were cocoonlike pupae, brown nutlike nodes, some trailing thin white wisps of weaving stuff.

Acting on a hunch, Pete scanned the other chambers. They, too, were stocked with eggs, pilfered from the hopper. There were newly hatched larvae and dozens of pupae nodes.

Stepping back from the glass nest, Pete saw that it seethed with motion in all its parts. It was crawling with larvae. Worker ants were in constant motion.

Down at the hopper, ants wrestled out another egg, handing it off to others, who hauled it away.

"Thieving crumbs! Stealing my eggs . . . !"

Pete was burned. He said: "It'd take all day to get those eggs, and I'd have to tear up the whole nest to do it—which might not be a bad idea!"

The ants had put one over on him.

"I don't like that," he said.

He thumped his fingertips against the glass, opposite some ants who were carrying away an egg.

"Drop it."

He thumped harder.

"Come on, drop it, you jerks!"

The thumping caused a part of the tunnel ahead of them to collapse. The ants backed up, dragging the egg. One went forward and began digging, tunneling through the collapsed area.

She cleared the blockage. The ants went back to carrying away their prize.

Collecting jar in hand, Pete went to the second nest, the one in the middle.

This, too, had had its hopper all but emptied.

Pete shook his head slowly. "Do you believe this? What is this, the day the ants got wise?"

He went to the third nest on the right. This time the hopper was at least half-full of copper pellets, a welcome sight.

Some of those new jumbo eggs studded the pile.

"Now, that's more like it," Pete said, smiling.

He held the collecting jar in place, its mouth under the bottom of the funnel gate.

He thumbed a small handle in the base of the nest, causing a metal plate to slide over the top of the funnel, sealing it off. That guarded against the queen getting out.

Of course, the queens never seemed to want to get out. They were forted up, each in her chambers, ringed by worker attendants. The workers fed them and tended to the eggs.

Pete tapped his fingernail against the glass, opposite where the queen squatted, atop a pile of eggs.

She recoiled, antennae whipsawing. Worker ants swarmed her, surrounding her, moving her away from the disturbance.

Not too far away, just to another part of the chamber. It would take a real emergency to cause the queen to abandon the chamber.

Pete opened the hopper's release gate. Eggs dropped down the slide, toward the jar.

Too late, Pete saw that a few ants had gotten among the eggs. That had happened before, and it was no big deal. He would just pick the ants out of the eggs and crush them. He had more than enough ants.

This time, though, the ants were quicker.

About a half dozen were salted in with the eggs. A couple fell into the jar, but the others managed to scramble onto the lip of the jar mouth.

They ran across the glass lip onto Pete's hand.

Where they stayed.

And dug in.

First, they sank their sharp-pointed, hooked mandible jaws into his flesh, biting deep.

That hurt, but it was only a prelude, anchoring them to Pete so they could really put a hurting on him.

They went to work with their stingers.

It happened faster than it takes to tell it. They were very quick, very sure. They didn't have to think about what they were doing. It was hardwired instinct, the attack response.

One of them was a type of ant that Pete had

never seen before. It was full-grown, wasp-sized, a type known as the Myrmex hoplite major.

Its fore end seemed all jaws, and its tail seemed all stinger. It was what was commonly known not as a worker ant, but as a soldier.

The breed was regaining some of its primeval vigor, sprouting into the crude, vigorous, voracious hoplites that had wreaked havoc during the Age of Reptiles.

Jeez, that's a big one, Shannon thought to himself, in the instant the hoplite major hopped on to his hand.

It squatted over the base of his thumb, facing him.

A few others, of the smaller dwarf type, also clung to his hand, but it was the major that had his attention.

The major dug in, chomping down with her choppers.

As if that were a signal, the others dug in, too.

It hurt!

Pete was breathless with the shock of it, like a man plunged into cold water. He couldn't catch his breath to yell.

The ants went to work with their stingers.

"YEEEEEEOWWWWWWW!"

9

THE ANTS DIDN'T JUST STING ONCE, AND THEN forget about it. They stung six, eight, ten times in quick succession.

Pete let go of the jar. It fell on the floor but didn't break.

He shook his hand, trying to lose the ants. They wouldn't let go. Worse, they kept stinging.

Those stings lanced into him like red-hot hat pins.

His eyes were bulging out of his head. He was electrified with pain and fear.

He smashed the back of his hand against the worktable, grinding the ants into jelly against the boards.

He turned his hand as he rubbed, making sure to get them all.

"Ah," he said.

He held up his hand. Ants were smeared across the back of it. In some places, there were bits of paste mixed with blood, with antennae sticking out of the pile, or sticklike legs, and they were twitching.

Pete gripped the wrist of his bitten hand.

A sob of pain caught in his throat as he called the ants a bunch of dirty names.

His hand was red, throbbing.

Remembering the collecting jar, he looked down.

The jar lay on its side, having somehow survived the fall intact. Some eggs had spilled on the floor.

Among them were a few ants, scurrying around in different directions. Luckily, they hadn't gotten too far yet.

Cursing feelingly under his breath, he trampled the ants, smearing them underfoot.

Just when he thought he'd gotten them all, a searing pain lanced his left ankle.

"Oww!"

Reeling, he clawed at his pants legs, pulling it up. Clinging to a patch of bare skin, above the top of his sock, was a stinging ant. It was a dwarf worker, but it still hurt like blazes.

He scraped it with the heel of his other shoe, smearing it.

Another bite. He fought back a groan.

He checked to make sure there were no more ants, hiding in his socks or anywhere else. There weren't.

"Lousy no-good ants . . . !"

A knock sounded on the bolted door, slow, hesitant.

"Pete?" Annie said.

"What?" he said, through clenched teeth.

"You okay?"

"No!"

"What?"

"I'm okay," he lied. "What do you want?"

"I heard you yell."

"I dropped something."

"You must have dropped a lead weight on your foot, the way you were hollering."

"Never mind. What are you, nuts, leaving a cash register unattended? You crazy?"

From behind the door, her voice sounded thin, tired. "There's no customers in the store, Pete."

"One could've come in," he said. "What are you doing back here, anyway?"

"I wanted to make sure you were all right."

"Go back to your register."

"Okay," she said.

She went away. Now that she was gone, Pete realized that he missed the distraction. It had kept him from concentrating on his hand.

It was redder and more swollen. There were three red dots, each one thumbtack-sized, where the lesser ants had stung.

Where the major had stung him, at the base

of the thumb, there was an ugly purple-red mark, as big as a dime. It looked bruised.

There were other, smaller sets of red marks where he had been bitten.

He was hurt. And scared. And not just scared for the present, either.

Suppose the ants should get loose from their Ant Castles, stinging some of the kids who'd sent away for them?

"Jeez, their folks would sue me into the ground," Pete said.

And they would get loose, some of them, at least. Kids were always doing something stupid, breaking their toys, and the Ant Castles weren't built so good in the first place. They wouldn't hold up to much abuse, and maybe not even to normal wear and tear.

He'd planned to be out of the business with a nice profit before the returns and complaints started.

But he'd underestimated the ants, totally.

"How was I supposed to know they'd sting?" he said.

If he had known, he'd have made sure that at least he wouldn't get stung.

And the ants were tricky. The way they'd hidden in the hopper, lying in wait among the eggs, then rushing out in a bold, suicidal assault—

Why, it was almost as if they'd planned it that way!

But that was ridiculous. Ants don't make plans and lay ambushes.

His aching hand said different.

These ants were dangerous. They were a menace!

Pete glared at the nests, openly hating.

"For two cents, I'd bomb you with insecticide and wash my hands of you," he said.

In all three glass nests, the ants teemed, seething.

When did there get to be so many of them?

It was more than a little bit frightening.

10

"LETHAL LARVAE," ROBBIE SAID, IMPRESSED. "All right!"

It was an hour or so after dinner. The meal of spicy meat and other heavy foods that Mrs. Cunningham had cooked lay thick on his stomach, but that was forgotten in the wonderment at seeing the grubs that had so quickly sprouted from the eggs in the tray of water.

About a third of them had already hatched, their shredded egg cases littering the sandy floor of the cube.

Copper-colored, wormlike crawlers inched around in the dirt. In the tray, the remaining egg pellets throbbed and pulsed, quickening with life.

"I guess it's not a gyp after all," Robbie said.

He unwrapped a napkin. In it were some oily flecks of meat, which he had filched from the dinner table when Mrs. Cunningham wasn't looking.

The instructions had said that the larvae, and the ants, thrived best on such a diet.

He used his fingers to shred the meat into strands. Even then, they looked too big for the grubs, almost as big as they were.

Opening the hatch on the lid of the nest, he sprinkled in the scraps.

The crawlers had started to react even before he had reached for the hatch, lifting their front ends off the dirt and raising them into the air, as if sensing the nearness of food.

When he opened the hatch, almost all the grubs raised themselves up, looking like microsnakes poised to strike.

The meaty scraps hit the floor of the nest. The crawlers swarmed them. Holes opened in the tips of their smooth, featureless snouts. They fastened on the meat and began munching.

"They sure are hungry," Robbie said admiringly.

In quick time, the scraps lessened and the grubs grew, visibly swelling from the bulk of the meat they ate.

There was a fascinating nastiness to their mindless hunger. They ate until they were full, swollen, stuffed to bursting. Until they couldn't eat another bite.

Then they were slow, lazy. They lay in place

for long minutes at a time, and when they moved, it was at half power.

There had been more meat than they could handle at one feeding. The remnants lay in place, mobbed by the grubs. Even when they were too full to eat, they liked to be around the food. They stretched out on top of the scraps, rolling around on them, rubbing themselves until they were coated with food oils.

In the tray, the end of a copper egg was split by the tip of a snout. Another larva was hatching.

It pushed its way out of the egg, like toothpaste being squeezed out of a tube.

When it had fully emerged, its pale copper form was wet and glistening. Its strugglings had caused the egg to roll to the bottom of the tray. The number of eggs had already decreased by a third, but there was almost no water left in the tray. This was because the eggs had absorbed most of the water, through their pores.

The newborn climbed up the eggs, inching toward the top of the pile. It bellied over the edge of the tray, falling down into the dirt.

It started crawling, inching toward the meat scraps. As soon as it reached one, it fastened onto it and started chewing.

"They're like little monsters," Robbie said. "I

wonder if they'd eat each other? Maybe if there was no other food . . . ?"

In the tray, another egg stirred, from the quickening within.

The doorknob rattled.

Robbie started, turning around in the chair that he had set up in front of the desk so he'd have a ringside seat while watching the Ant Castle that sat on the desktop.

"What?" he said, irritated at the interruption.

On the other side of the door was Mrs. Cunningham. He'd been so absorbed in the Lethal Larvae that he hadn't heard her coming up the stairs and down the hall.

"Robbie?"

"What?" he repeated, even more irritated.

"Why is your door locked, dear?"

"For privacy."

"What are you doing in there?"

"My homework."

"Why do you need the door locked for that?"

"Because it breaks my concentration when people come barging in and interrupting me."

"Oh. Well, I'll only be a moment. Could you open the door, please?"

If he didn't, she'd just keep hanging around in the hall, not going away.

He glanced at the Ant Castle. If she saw the

crawlers squirming around, she was sure to make a fuss.

They were too cool for her not to.

"Robbie? May I speak to you for a moment, please?"

"Go ahead."

"It's polite to look somebody in the face when you address them. Open the door, please, dear."

He was busy, moving the Ant Castle to the back of his desk, against the wall, out of the light. He pushed a pile of books in front of it. They weren't big enough to cover it, so he added on a few more from another pile.

That did the trick. He put a couple of comic books on top of the pile, for extra coverage.

"Robbie."

"All right, I'm coming!"

Stepping back, he took a last look. The cube with its wriggling grubs was well hidden.

He went to the door, unlocked and opened it.

Mrs. Cunningham was there, a big smile pasted on her face. It didn't reach her eyes. They were sharp, narrowed, watchful. They were in constant motion, peering beyond him into the room, looking for something out of place, out of line, that would indicate that the youngster had been up to some sort of mischief behind the locked door.

What kind of mischief, she was unsure, but she had her dark suspicions. What did she see? Only the desk, heaped with piles of books, and the desk lamp lit, and the chair pushed away from the desk, as if Robbie had been sitting there and moved it to answer the door, as indeed he had.

"You must be the antisocial type," she said, trying for lightness.

"That's what the school shrink said." He was serious, unsmiling.

She would have liked to come for a closer look, but he stood in the way, so she couldn't enter without shoving him aside; she was thwarted.

She sniffed the air, nostrils wrinkling in disapproval. "Stuffy in here."

"I don't mind, Mrs. Cunningham."

"You should leave the door open, for better circulation."

"The windows are open," he said, smiling thinly. "Uh, I was studying. Was there something you wanted?"

"Why, yes. Do you know where the TV program guide is?"

"It should be downstairs, in the TV room."

"Oh. I didn't see it."

"It's usually on top of the coffee table."

"I didn't see it there."

"It was there the last time I saw it."

She shrugged.

"Maybe it's under some magazines. Or on the shelf, under the table with the lamp," he said.

"Well, I'll take another look."

"Good."

"Do you think Gwen might have taken it?"

"No. And I wouldn't go in her room to look for it, Mrs. Cunningham. Gwen doesn't like it when people go there uninvited."

Her smile was wintry. "Yes, she made that quite clear."

He fidgeted, glancing impatiently at his desk. "I've got a lot of homework, Mrs. Cunningham."

"Such a diligent young man, so eager to get back to your studies. Such dedication is highly commendable."

"I've got to get good grades so I can get into a top school." He said this with a straight face.

She looked at her watch. "You've got plenty of time left for your books. After all, your bedtime isn't until ten o'clock."

"Eleven!" he shouted. "Mom and Dad allow me to stay up until eleven on weeknights!"

"Oh, yes, that's right. I forgot." Her smile said, *Gotcha!*

She'd known how to press his buttons.

"I'll look in on you later, Robbie. Don't work too hard."

"Um."

She went away. He closed the door and locked it. He stood there, listening to her going downstairs.

After a pause, there was the sound of the TV being turned on in the TV room. That should keep her busy for a while.

She was old, and didn't much like climbing stairs, so that should help keep her out of his hair. For a while.

He went back to the cube. It looked like a few more grubs had hatched while he was busy with Mrs. Cunningham.

At a few minutes before ten o'clock, Gwen came home. With the windows open, Robbie heard the McBane brothers' heavy-engined muscle car coming from a long way off.

Mrs. Cunningham heard it, too, but then, she was listening for it. At the first rumbles, she was up out of her chair in the TV room and across the front hall, so she could stand watching at the window.

The car pulled up in front of the house and stood there for a minute. There was the sound of male and female voices, laughter, and music from the radio. The engine kept running.

The car door opened and Gwen stepped out onto the pavement. A light went on in the car, showing the brothers and the Trent twins.

The door closed, blacking out the car interior.

Gwen stood with her hand on the car door, chatting with her friends for a while longer.

Meanwhile Robbie was doing some hard thinking.

Gwen was surprisingly flexible, expecially for a big sister. She generally tolerated what she called his "weirdnesses," as long as they weren't too obnoxious, and didn't get in her face.

Her tolerance had its limits, though, and he knew that the Ant Castle was well beyond them.

"It's the Lethal Larvae," he said. "She won't stay under the same roof with them. No girl would. And, since she won't leave, they'll have to go. On something like that, she might even team up with Mrs. Cunningham. They'd probably make me keep them in the garage, or outside.

"Heck with that. I want these babies where I can see them. Anyway, they'll change into ants soon, and that won't be so bad. I can get away with keeping the ants. It's the larvae that are the problem."

Footsteps sounded on the front walk, nearing. The door opened, and Gwen entered.

By this time Mrs. Cunningham had again retreated to the TV room. She stood there in the doorway, as if she had just gotten up when she heard Gwen coming.

It didn't work; Gwen had seen her silhouetted against the window when she had been peeking out of it.

She didn't let on that she knew, though. She turned, waving good-bye to her friends.

The red car drove away.

After some polite, meaningless chitchat with Mrs. Cunningham, Gwen went upstairs.

She knocked on Robbie's door. He unlocked and opened it.

There was color in her face, her eyes were bright, and she smelled fresh and green, as if she'd brought scent of the night air with her.

She said, "How's everything going with you-know-who?" Her voice was pitched low so it wouldn't carry.

He shrugged. "What's with the vegetarian bit?"

"Oh, that."

"She was going on about it at dinner. Since when did you become a vegan, Gwen?"

"Since she started cooking here."

"It's not so bad."

"Please."

"Anyway, I picked up on it, so I covered for you."

"What did you say?"

"Nothing. I said yeah, you're a vegan."

"That's a good boy."

"You owe me."

"Hey, I thought we were sticking together against her."

"Oh, yeah, right. Okay."

"She's such a pest!" Gwen said feelingly.

"Mom and Dad called."

"Oh? How's their trip?"

"Okay. They said they were sorry that they missed talking to you, because they were out."

"I know. You-know-who told me, trying to guilt-trip me," Gwen said. "Mom and Dad can be pests, too," she added. "In a nice way, I mean."

She glanced idly about the room, without curiosity.

The Ant Castle was not in sight. Robbie had hidden it under the desk, way out of sight.

Her gaze flicked across the empty box and packaging, part of which was sticking out of the wastebasket.

He'd forgotten about that.

"How's your new toy?"

"It's not a toy, it's an Ant Castle," he said.

"Ants." She shook her head. "You are too weird. Where is it?"

"I didn't put it together yet. It's a hassle. There's a lot of small pieces you have to fit together. I couldn't concentrate with Mrs. Cunningham hanging around."

Gwen nodded. "I know what you mean. Where are the ants?"

"Huh?"

"Where are the ants, from the ant thing?"

"Ant Castle," he said.

"Whatever. Where are they? If they're not in the thing, where are they? They better not get out, Robbie."

"There aren't any ants."

She was skeptical. "What? No ants in an Ant Castle?"

"Ask Mrs. Cunningham if you don't believe me. She looked at it, and there weren't any ants."

"I believe you. But what's an Ant Castle without ants?"

"You have to supply the ants yourself. Dig up an anthill and put it inside the Ant Castle."

"Why?"

"So you can watch the ants."

"Why not watch them at the anthill?"

"Because the Ant Castle has clear sides so you can see the whole nest."

"Why do you want to do that?"

"I'm into science."

"Robbie, you are too weird. If you bring ants into the house, you better make sure they don't get out."

"Now who's the pest?" he demanded.

"You're right. It must be catching. Well, good night."

"Good night."

"Thank goodness the guest room is downstairs, so you-know-who doesn't have to sleep up here!"

"She comes up a lot anyhow."

"I bet," she said. "See you."

" 'Night."

"Too weird," Gwen said to herself, shaking her head as she went to her room. "I've got to put up with you-know-who, and a buggy brother. Too much!"

There'd be more.

11

"YOU GUYS ARE REALLY FAST!"

Robbie spoke to the larvae, who lay thick on the cube's sandy floor.

It was morning, time to get up and get ready to go to school. Mrs. Cunningham had already been up for a long time. Gwen was in the bathroom, taking a shower.

Robbie, wearing pants and an undershirt, knelt on the floor in front of the desk. He had just hauled the Ant Castle out from the back of the kneehole space, into the open.

The cube sat on the floor in front of him. He knelt facing it, head bowed, palms flat on the floor on either side of the cube. It looked like he was praying to it.

Overnight, all the eggs had hatched, and not one unbroken copper pellet remained in the tray.

The larvae crawled in the dirt, on each other,

along the smooth clear sides of the cube. There were a lot of them, and they were active.

Maybe they were hungry. He reached for the greasy rumpled napkin, which held the remnants of yesterday's meat scraps.

They had dried, turning stiff and hard. He tore them in half, like paper matches. He sprinkled them through the top hatch, into the cube.

The crawlers became frantic, wriggling like tadpoles. They fastened on the scraps in a food frenzy.

"Wow. Wonder what they'd do if I stuck my finger in there?"

It was an experiment he was unwilling to try. Maybe he could get somebody else to put their finger in. But who? Not Gwen, or Mrs. Cunningham. They and the crawlers must be kept apart, never to meet.

His friends? He didn't have many, and they were the same kind of smart-alecky, wise kids as he, the type who'd try to get the other guy to offer up his finger for the cause.

If he stuck a pencil in there, would they go for that?

There was no time for such scientific explorations. He had stuff to do.

According to the instructions, once the larvae had hatched, it was time to fill the cube with dirt.

With Gwen in the shower, and Mrs. Cunningham making breakfast in the kitchen, now was the time to act.

Robbie put the cube on his desk. He took the rubber band off the bag of soil and unwrapped it.

The meat scraps were gone. The hungry crawlers had gobbled them down, and were now bulging with the bulk of the mass inside them.

"You guys can sure put it away," he said.

The sound of the shower being turned off was a spur to action. There was still some time, since Gwen liked to fuss forever with her hair and makeup.

He held a top corner of the bag over the open top hatch of the cube, hesitating. He was supposed to pour in the dirt, right on top of the larvae, piling it up.

That's what the instructions said to do. It wouldn't hurt the crawlers. Underground was their natural environment. They were tunnelers. The soil would hold enough air for them to breathe, and they would absorb useful nutrients through it, through their skins.

He poured in the dirt, sifting it slowly at

first. It fell like tan rain on the swarming wrigglers.

It felt like burying them alive.

But, that's what the instructions said to do. The crawlers would get to work and soon have it honeycombed with chambers and tunnels, the infrastructure of the ant-colony nest.

A puff of dust rose out of the top hatch as the soil level climbed in the cube.

When the bag was emptied, the cube was filled almost all the way, with a few inches of space between the dirt and the lid.

That was where he'd place the food scraps, on the surface of the dirt, where the crawlers and, soon, the ants would tunnel up to it.

He couldn't see any crawlers, though. Just dirt. He saw movement, and thought it might be larvae, but it was just the soil settling.

After a minute, though, he could make out a few wriggling copper forms, squirming in the dirt, pressing against the sides of the cube.

"All right. There's no stopping you guys," Robbie said.

He closed the top hatch, securing it with the safety catch. A not unpleasant scent of soil tickled his nostrils, making them itch.

He thought he was going to sneeze, but he didn't.

Where to put the Ant Castle?

Under the desk was good enough when he was in the room, able to stand off intruders, but it wouldn't do for the long hours while he was away at school, when Mrs. Cunningham would have the time to do some nice long leisurely snooping.

He hid the cube in his closet, at the back of a crowded top shelf. He moved other stuff around it, covering it, burying it from view.

The closet was cluttered and messy, and he didn't think that Mrs. Cunningham would be eager to probe too deeply into it.

That done, he finished getting dressed and went down for breakfast.

Mrs. Cunningham handled a skillet on top of the stove, making a big breakfast of sausage and eggs that only she would eat.

Gwen stood by the counter, eating cereal and milk out of a bowl.

Mrs. Cunningham crossed to a wall-mounted rack, where kitchen utensils hung from hooks. She reached for another skillet.

On her way back to the stove, she stopped, looking down at the floor, where a blot of motion was moving.

She placed a foot on it, and very deliberately ground it out of existence.

"An ant," she said.

She and Gwen stared Robbie in the face.

"Don't look at me. It's not one of mine," he said. "I don't have any," he added quickly.

He said it straight-faced, and he wasn't even lying. He didn't have any ants.

Larvae, yes. But no ants.

Not yet.

12

THE ANTS ANTS ANTS—

"What'd you say, Pete?" Annie said.

Pete looked blankly at her for half a minute before replying. "Huh?"

"You were saying something just now, but I didn't catch it," she said.

He shook his head, blinking bleary eyes. "Nothing. Never mind."

"You okay, Pete?"

"Sure," he croaked. "Why do you ask?"

"I don't know, you just seem, well, kind of tired, that's all," Annie said.

You look like a zombie, Pete, she said to herself. *One of the living dead.*

He looked bad, like he was coming off a three-day drunk and had a bad case of the shakes. Except that he didn't drink. He didn't smoke, either, or go out with women, or even eat too much red meat. His only vice was that he was a chiseler, out to separate the public from its dollars by every legal way possible, and a lot of ways that weren't so legal.

Plus, he had an unpleasant personality. But he didn't drink.

Normally, his appearance was as clean and sharp-edged as if it'd been stamped out by a machine.

Now his hair was uncombed, his eyes were bloodshot, and he needed a shave. His shirt collar and cuffs were dirty, his clothes rumpled. He was wearing the same clothes he'd worn yesterday. He'd been wearing them since then, around the clock without changing.

His face was pale, clammy. His right hand was wrapped in bandages, gauze bandages that covered it from fingertips to beyond the wrist, showing not an inch of skin. The hand was wrapped mitten-style, with the fingers all together, It looked like the hand of a mummy. Big, clumsy, it was twice the size of his unhurt left hand.

Because of the bandages, Annie thought.

Some fluids from inside had discolored the bandages with yellow stains. It smelled nasty, but Annie kept her distance from Pete, so that really wasn't a problem.

His talking to himself was. That bothered her, made her nervous.

Ever since she'd arrived at the Trading Post, earlier this Tuesday afternoon, coming here directly after school to put in her daily working hours, Pete Shannon had been acting strange.

He'd spent most of his time closeted in the back room, behind a closed door. That wasn't like him. He was a hands-on kind of manager, usually spending most of his time on the store floor, where he could keep an eye on Annie and the customers, making sure that they didn't get away with anything.

That was his style, but not today. On the first few times he came out of the back, he wandered around on the main floor, drifting from aisle to aisle. Purposeless.

He kept his right arm close to him, cradling his bandaged hand against his stomach.

He talked to himself, muttering under his breath. That was what he'd been doing a moment ago, when Annie had heard him and thought he was talking to her.

He wasn't. He was talking to himself, about *the ants.* What he said about them wasn't very nice, so it was a good thing that Annie couldn't hear him.

The ants ants ants—

What to do about them?

What *could* be done?

"What time is it, girl?"

When he said that, he was looking at the wall clock. At least, his face was turned toward it, even if he wasn't seeing it.

Annie noticed. It freaked her a little, but she was careful to humor the boss. So she told him the time that was on the clock.

"Uh, it's twenty minutes to six, Pete."

He didn't say anything, didn't respond, just kept looking at the clock.

"Pete?"

This time he turned his head, looking at her.

Under his eyes were big black rings of fatigue. He looked like a raccoon.

She repeated the time.

"Right," he said. "It's getting late."

She couldn't think of anything to say to that, so she didn't. She stood behind the counter, fidgeting. She glanced around, vaguely grateful for the presence of an elderly couple, shopping in the aisles.

It wouldn't be so much fun to be alone in the store with Pete.

Pete shook his head, as if to clear it. His eyes focused, losing some of that glazed look.

"It's getting late," he said.

He turned, abruptly leaving. With newfound

purpose, he marched down the aisle, vanishing into the back room.

After a pause a distant cry sounded:

"Lord!"

Annie started. Surely that had been Pete, groaning aloud. He sounded bad.

She glanced at the elderly couple. The oldsters browsed among the display items, murmuring, clucking over prices. They seemed undisturbed.

Maybe they hadn't heard the cry. They were closer to the back rooms than Annie, who was behind the counter at the front of the store. Why had she heard it, and not they?

Maybe she'd imagined it.

Or maybe they were hard of hearing. They wouldn't be the first oldsters who were And these too were right up there, age-wise. Regular geezers.

Annie, alert, listened for more outcries, but there were none.

Pete was a big boy. He could take care of himself. Maybe he'd stubbed his toe, and cried out. Or bumped his bad hand. Sure, that explained it.

Although the cry had seemed to be more one of shock than of pain. What she could recall of it. Which wasn't much, since it had come and gone so quickly.

And, she wasn't entirely sure that she hadn't imagined it.

"None of my business," she said out loud, shrugging.

Then she caught what she was doing.

"Now *I'm* talking to myself—oops! I just did it again!"

She put a hand to her mouth, closing it. The mouth, not the hand.

Five minutes later Pete reentered the scene. He came out of the back room, making a beeline for the oldsters.

He was almost on them when they finally looked up and saw him coming. They were examining the frog ashtrays, ceramic green-glazed frogs whose hollowed backs could double as ashtrays or candy serving dishes.

On the bottom of the frogs were the price stickers. The oldsters were picking up frogs and turning them upside down, making sour faces and tsk-tsking over the prices.

Pete loomed up on them, rushing along the aisle. He was head down, his face set, eyes blazing. He looked like he was going to run them down.

The old guy flinched. His wife recoiled, crying "Oh!" She raised white-gloved hands, holding them in front of her, making warding gestures. One hand was still clutching a frog.

Pete drew himself up, stopping a few feet short of a collision. He was breathing heavily.

"You'll have to leave," he said. "We're closing."

They stood there stunned, not reacting.

"Get out," he said.

The old man stiffened, as if struck. His wife paled, eyes widening. He took her arm, steering her away.

"Let's go, dear," he said.

She was glad to go. They went up the aisle, him holding her arm above the elbow, their white shoes striding briskly. Flustered, she still clutched the frog, unaware of it.

Pete walked behind, following on their heels. That kept them moving at a nice pace.

Annie stood amazed, not believing what she was seeing.

Pete Shannon chasing out a potential paying customer . . . ?!

Impossible! It went against human nature—his.

But it was real, it was happening.

The couple slowed as they neared the front of the store. Pete, right behind them, said, "Don't stop now, there's the door."

The old guy balked, digging in his heels. From the neck up, his face burned bright red.

"Now you listen here, mister," he began.

His wife tugged on his arm, trying to pull him away. "Don't argue with him, dear—

"He's drunk," she added, under her breath, but loud enough to be heard.

"Think what you like, outside," Pete said.

They started for the door. The old guy's hand was on the exit bar and he was pushing the door open, when Annie spoke.

"Hey, you gonna pay for that frog?"

She had to say it. Pete would have been sore if she hadn't. That's what she thought.

The woman had forgotten about the frog in her hand, so flustered was she at being rudely hustled out of the store.

Now she remembered. She reddened, embarrassed.

"Keep it," Pete said. "Just get out."

Annie was flabbergasted.

The woman, already humiliated at being tagged by the girl for trying to walk out with something without paying for it—though she acted innocently and absentmindedly—now became enraged.

She slapped the frog down hard on the counter, so hard that it sounded like a shot. A ceramic chip flew off.

Annie was sure that it had been broken, but amazingly, except for the chip, it was intact.

"Keep your awful old frog!" the woman said.

She and her husband marched out, chins held high. He paused in the open doorway, turning to have the last word.

"I'm going to complain to the local chamber of commerce," he said. "And the Better Business Bureau, too!" he added.

Then he was gone, he and the missus, scuttling across the gravel to a recreational vehicle parked nearby.

The RV started up, lumbered out of the lot, and drove away.

Pete stood at the door, watching. Annie knew better than to ask what it was all about. She didn't say anything. She hardly moved, not wanting to call the other's attention to her.

Pete made a curt nod of satisfaction, then turned his attention to the inside of the store.

Annie stiffened, not looking him in the face. She knew he was looking at her.

"Go home," he said.

Whatever she was expecting to hear, that wasn't it.

"Uh . . . huh?" she said.

He jerked a thumb at the door. "Out. Now. Get your coat and go."

She looked at the clock. It was about ten minutes to six. Official closing time was at seven.

"It's early yet," she said, frowning.

He laughed, without humor. "That's what you think. I'm closing up early tonight."

She stood in place, hesitating, more puzzled than anything else.

"Snap it up, girl. Get along."

She shrugged. "You're the boss."

"Am I? We'll see." As he spoke, he glanced back, toward the back rooms. He looked anxious, worried.

The mood passed. He looked at Annie, his anxiety gone, replaced by irritation.

"Hurry. I want to close before any more jerk customers show up," he said.

He was fidgeting, twitchy. Under other circumstances, his behavior might even have been called "antsy."

He circled the counter, crossing behind it and to the side, to a panel of switches set chest-high in the wall.

The switches controlled the lights. He started flicking them off.

In the store, banks of overhead lights went dark, shadowing the area below. Pete threw more switches, turning the barnlike interior into a checkerboard of light and darkness.

That stung Annie into action. She didn't want to be alone with Pete in the dark.

She reached under the counter, where she

had put her coat. She grabbed it, scooting out from behind the counter, darting past Pete, into open floor area.

She felt better, in the open, where there was nobody standing between her and the exit.

Pete stopped switching off the lights, turning away from the panel.

He started toward her.

"I'm gone," she said, heading for the door. Not running, but not idling, either.

He followed, not chasing, just following to make sure she went out, as he had done with the oldsters.

To her retreating back, he said, "You'll have to get a ride home. I'm staying."

"Sure," she said, not slackening.

"I've got some business to take care of. Important business."

"Okay. Bye," she said, going out the door.

Outside, sunlight and open air burst upon her. After the weirdness in the store, it was dizzying, like coming out of a darkened movie house into the bright light of day.

It was warm, and there was traffic on the highway. Annie kept walking, not looking back.

When she was halfway across the lot, she glanced back over her shoulder, just in time to see Pete moving away from the door, disappearing inside.

She stopped, scratching her head. "Pete's really warping out."

Usually, he gave her a ride home after work. Now you couldn't pay her to get in a car with him behind the wheel.

She shook her head. "If I didn't know better, I'd think he was on something. But he's the type who wouldn't even take an aspirin if he had a headache.

"Whatever's bugging him, it's sure no headache. Maybe his hand is hurting bad. Wonder how he hurt it?"

In the west, the sun was still over the horizon. There was still some time left before the cars had to put on their lights, but there were shadows on the land. Soft purple shadows, in the hollows of the woodsy landscape.

Annie was a long way from home, too far to walk. She could walk it if she had to, but that would take hours, so it was really only a last-case option.

She needed a ride. At a corner of the lot, to one side of the entrance, stood a pay phone.

Annie went to it, preceded by a long shadow. The sun was low, and shadows were long.

It was too early for her mother to be home,

but she had no one else to call, so she called home.

No answer.

She hung up, pocketing the change. She would call later. She sat on a low metal fence, beside the phone.

Cars passed, fewer now that the modest commuter rush had passed. It was dinnertime.

Falling light made objects stand out clearly. Every weed, every rock and pebble in the lot stood out in sharp-edged detail, like a photograph.

Annie frowned, disturbed. Something was missing. She felt undressed, incomplete.

She was suffering a lack of—what?

It nagged at her for a moment, then she got it. Or, rather, she hadn't got it.

Her backpack.

She'd left it in the store. Now she remembered. Usually, she kept it in the same place as her coat, under the counter. Today, though, when she'd come in, she'd gotten distracted by a customer, and stowed it in the nearest place handy, a shelf in the wall behind the counter.

Later, when she'd gone out, she'd grabbed her coat and gone, forgetting the bag.

Remembering, she stood up, staring at the store, seeing only its blank front.

"I need that bag," she said.

In it were some schoolbooks, for tonight's studies. She always did her studies. Hard work and studying were the only things that were going to get her out of the rut. Without an education, she'd be stuck in the same hole as the rest of her family.

Plus, there was other stuff in the bag, personal stuff.

"It's mine and I want it. And I'm not leaving without it," she said.

Taking a deep breath, she started back toward the store.

13

PETE SHANNON STOOD OUTSIDE THE CLOSED back room door, leaning against the wall, unwrapping his bandaged hand.

Alone. He was alone now. The girl was gone and he was alone. Alone, with his little problem.

Inside, the store was still a crazy quilt, stitched together with patches of light and darkness, the random pattern of the electric lights he'd switched off.

Once he'd seen that Annie was on her way and not coming back, he'd staggered back into the depths of the store, not bothering with the lights.

In the back room, the lights were on. They shone above the tops of the partitioned walls and under the door.

He wouldn't leave that room in the dark, not for a second.

He leaned against the wall, needing the support. He was weak, rubbery in the knees.

He was holding his bandaged hand in front of him. It throbbed. Each time it throbbed, he felt it in his hand, like his heart was stuffed inside his skull with his brain, crowding it, hammering it with every beat.

He studied the bandaged hand. It seemed bigger than before, swollen to the size of an oven mitt.

It was getting worse, not better.

He had to see it. With his left hand, his fingers found and plucked at the end of the bandages, the topmost wrapping. They were clumsy and he moved carefully, not wanting to jar his bad hand. The skin felt stretched to bursting, a giant magnifying membrane that made the slightest touch feel like agony.

He freed the end of the strip, unwinding it. Loop by loop, strand by strand, the long gauze wrappings came undone, ribboning to the floor at his feet.

Then it was done and the hand was bared, exposed.

It no longer resembled an oven mitt. Now it looked like a work glove, stuffed until the seams were near bursting.

A purple glove. Dark purple, plum-colored. At the wrist, the color faded to a bruised, brownish red.

The fingers were as big as sausages.

The back of the hand was marked with puncture wounds, as if a dozen or so nails had been driven into it, then pulled out.

"Ants did a job on me," he muttered.

He said something dirty.

His hand was grotesque, a monstrosity. Ant bites had done that to him. Stings. Especially from that big brute soldier ant.

There was something in those stings, too, some toxin. Poison, like a bee sting, only worse, much worse. Or maybe, if he'd taken as many bee stings in one place, his hand would be just as bad.

He didn't know. Or care.

Whatever it was, he couldn't go for treatment, not yet. Doctors and emergency wards keep records. A case like this would be sure to stand out.

He didn't want to be linked to any case of severe insect bites. Before too long, there was liable to be a lot of such cases, and he didn't want to leave any evidence connecting him to them.

There was too much of that already on the record.

Well, he could fix that. And would. Immediately.

His hand was ugly. He couldn't bear to look

at it. It was obscene. He shouldn't have uncovered it.

The wrappings were pooled on the floor, as if a mummy had shed some of its "skin." He could never untangle it and get it back on his hand.

He looked around, spotting a rack of T-shirts. He tore one off a hanger. A Cleveland Rock and Roll Hall of Fame T-shirt. He draped it over his hand, wrapping it loosely.

He could work better, now that he no longer had to look at it. Now he could do what had to be done.

He reached for the back room door with his good hand, pausing when he saw that the padlock hung open, unfastened.

He had forgotten to lock it earlier, the last time he'd come out. A bad mistake. Anyone could have walked right in—

He was slipping. Careless, making mistakes. It was the toxins from the stings. The poison was in his bloodstream, affecting his brain.

It fogged his mind, so he couldn't think straight. Like his mind kept going in and out of focus. When it went out, the picture blurred and he stumbled around like a drunken sleepwalker.

"I'm in focus now, you dirty ant so-and-sos—"

The rest were curse words.

He pushed open the door, lurching into the back room.

There was an impression of furious motion, seething activity. There was a sharp smell—reek, really—of acid, biting, bringing tears to the eyes.

There were creaking sounds.

They came from the glass nests, all three of them. Glass-sided walls bowed, bulging outward. Inside, things were pushing outward, with tremendous pressure.

The creakings were the sound of the glass panes straining against the metal frames.

There were scrabbling sounds.

Pete stepped back, involuntarily throwing his good arm in front of his face.

The nests were full to the point of overflowing, with masses of newly hatched ants.

Big bad ants, copper-colored ones. And so many!

Overnight, they had multiplied beyond belief. Last night, while he'd sweated out the long sleepless hours of fear and pain, they had been busy, increasing their numbers.

Beyond multiples, beyond geometric progressions, they had just kept making more of themselves. A graph of their growth would be an arrow climbing virtually straight up.

It was unnatural, such breeding powers. In the nests, tunnels and chambers had collapsed, swamped by sheer weight of numbers. Masses of ants and dirt.

There was dirt on the floor, lines of dust that had leaked out between the metal frames and glass walls of the nests.

A danger sign. At least, the creakings had stopped, if only for a moment. The walls had withstood the latest onslaught. The ants were resting, regrouping for the next attempt.

"I'll get you first," Pete said.

In a corner, under an old piece of canvas tarp, were some one-gallon plastic jugs, grouped together.

Pete uncovered them, moving them one at a time to the center of the room, near the door.

The jugs were full of liquid. Pete unscrewed one of their caps. There was a sharp smell of gasoline.

The jugs were filled with gas. They had plastic thumb loops at the necks for easier handling.

They weren't gas cans. They were plastic water bottles, filled with gas.

"No telltale metal gas cans to clue in the arson squad," Pete said.

He didn't know if he was talking to himself, or the ants, or both. The talking helped. Helped keep him in focus.

Picking up the opened jug, he began splashing it around, spilling gas around the room.

It was slow going, with only one good hand. His bad hand hurt too much to use. It was easier to pour the gas than splash it. He poured it over tables, benches, shelves, the floor.

Everything was wood. It would all burn.

"Fast and hot," he said.

The ants had been quiet, watchful, as if waiting to see what he would do. Once he started pouring the gas, they went back to work.

Creakings sounded from the nests.

Pete looked up from what he was doing, glaring. "Don't like that, do you? You know what I'm doing. Smart!

"There never was any ants like you. Devil ants, that's what you are. The devil with you!

"I've already sent out dozens of Ant Castles, dozens! All of them filled with devil ants like you! And when they hatch, what then?

"They'll turn on their owners, like you did me! Somebody's liable to get killed, and a lot of somebodies are sure to get hurt, and who's going to be left holding the bag? *Me!*"

He worked faster now. The jug was emptying and weighed less, making it easier to handle. Now he splashed more than he poured.

"An honest mistake, that's all. Anybody can make one. How was I supposed to know that you were ants from hell? I didn't know until it was too late.

"Well, Pete Shannon's got a few tricks of his own. Didn't think of that, did you, you dirty so-and-sos? You'll burn. The store, too, but that can't be helped. The evidence will be destroyed in the fire. Most of it, anyway. Enough to buy me some time to disappear.

"I'll empty my bank accounts, get lost in another state, far from here. Then I'll see a doctor, get fixed up.

"I'll be starting all over again, almost from scratch, but it's better than sitting in a prison cell. Which is where I'll be, if the cops ever catch Mr. Ant Castle.

"If I don't get lynched by some outraged parents whose kids get attacked by devil ants, first."

A groan sounded, from stressed metal. It was louder than the creakings, which were loud.

It was deep, ominous.

Pete froze. The groan had sounded like something was about to give. He held his breath, in an agony of suspense, waiting for a follow-up.

There was a shunting sound, as of a heavy weight slipping back into place. A glass wall, near to dislodging under the pressure of the ants, which had shifted, but held.

For how long?

Suddenly, Pete realized he had a lot less

time than he'd thought he had. The ants were near to breaking jail, quite near.

He worked faster, accidentally slopping some gas on his pants leg, leaving dark stains.

That scared and sobered him. He was more careful, emptying the rest of the jug.

Happily, he didn't have to do the same with the others. The remaining jugs sat grouped in the middle of the floor, facing the three slab-sided nests.

The last of the gas in the jug was used to make a trail to the other jugs.

Pete crouched over them, upending the jug, draining the last few drops. He let go of the empty bottle, straightening up.

"When the flames reach them, these jugs will go off like a firebomb. A fire hot enough to send you back to the hell you came from," he said.

He shook a fist at the nests, defiant.

"Devil ants!"

He reached into his pants pocket, fumbling, fishing out a lighter. He tried to flick it, to make sure it worked. It had checked out okay when he had tested it the previous night, but this was now.

He had trouble working it with his left hand. He thumbed the wheel, unable to start a light.

In the midst of his thumbings, a flame was

struck, surprising him, so that he almost dropped the lighter.

Then he thought of what a loose flame could have done to the masses of gasoline dousing the place, and got scared.

Sweat beaded on his face, cold sweat, as he took a very careful hold of the lighter.

"Whew! That was a close one. All I have to do now is light a torch, toss it—and good-bye!"

On the worktable were some rolled-up newspapers, which he'd brought for the purpose. He reached for one, picking it up.

Of course, he'd be standing at the door when he lit the paper, holding a good head start before he threw in the torch.

"When you meet your boss, the devil, tell him I said hello!"

Before he could begin to move away—

Kraaaaaaaaak.

A sound like ice breaking up at the start of a thaw.

Kraaak.

A jagged line ran down the center of the glass wall of the middle nest, the one directly facing Pete.

The nests were built to professional grades, from scientific supply houses. That was why they had lasted as long as they did. Had they been of the pet-store variety, they would have ended long ago.

Instead of now, as they were doing.

The glass slab splintered, shot through with spidery cracks. No longer clear, it was frosted, like powdered sugar.

To the left and right, in stereo, came the crackling sounds of the other nests giving way.

In an instant the slabs disintegrated.

Opposite Pete, the middle nest exploded, showering him with broken glass.

The nests were made of treated safety glass, so when they came apart, they burst into tiny cubes, like mini–ice cubes, instead of razor-sharp shredding shards.

The glass broke under the pressure of the sheer bulk of the masses of ants—after first having been weakened by streams of acidic venom, squirted on it by the ants.

It was more than coincidence that all three nests crumbled at the same time.

Pete threw up his arms in front of his face, to protect himself from showering glass.

The glass was nothing, compared with the ants. Like a spring that has been compressed, then released, the ant mass erupted into space, a living curtain.

It fell on Pete, wrapping him.

Screaming, he fell to the floor, into the jugs of gas, upsetting them, sending them sprawling.

One fell on its side, minus its cap, gushing pools of gasoline on the floor.

Freed from the flanking nests, the other ants piled on.

14

ANNIE STOOD OUTSIDE THE STORE, LOOKING in. Pete was nowhere to be seen. She guessed he was in the back room. That was where he'd been spending most of his time lately.

Doing what? She wasn't sure she cared to know. Something nasty, no doubt. Whatever it was, it wasn't doing him any good.

The door was unlocked. She could see that from outside. The square dead bolt hadn't been thrown.

The store was wide open. Anyone could walk right in.

"Pete's really losing it," she said.

She hesitated, waiting to see if he'd come out. Minutes passed without him emerging from that back room.

She couldn't wait forever. If she yelled, he might hear and come out. She wasn't thrilled at the thought of seeing him again, not when he was acting so weirded out.

A lot less hassle if she just slipped inside and went behind the counter and got her bag and left. It would only take about thirty seconds. She knew where the bag was.

And she wouldn't have to relate to Pete again. Which was cool, since he had kind of been giving her the creeps.

That decided her. She went inside.

Behind, the heavy glass door closed softly, eased by powerful cushioned springs.

She stood to one side of the counter, in the open area at the head of the aisles.

The store's cavernous space was checkered with boxes of light and dark, thanks to the haphazard way in which some electric lights were left burning, and others not.

The backroom door was ajar, venting light from within, spilling it on the floor outside.

That door was always left closed, always. Another sign that the boss was losing it. Annie shook her head.

After a minute she went behind the counter. Sure enough, her bag was where she thought she'd left it, a red nylon backpack with well-padded shoulder straps.

As she bent to pick it up, Annie realized what she'd look like if Pete should suddenly come upon her. He'd probably think she had sneaked in, to rob the cash register.

The thought had never entered her mind,

but she knew how Pete's mind worked, and it sure would enter his.

She felt guilty, as if she'd been committing a crime.

Noises came from the back room, changing guilt to fear.

She froze. More noise came from the back room, but Pete didn't come out.

The noises stopped.

Annie's heart once again started beating. She unfroze, scooting out from behind the counter.

Suddenly, from the back room:

Breaking glass. A few quick, choked screams, abruptly cut off.

Pete didn't scream much. Ants swarmed into his open mouth, a long thorny arm stuffed down his throat.

He was doomed, and he knew it. He wouldn't even have time to suffocate. The mega-doses of toxins he'd absorbed from hundreds of stingings, all at once, would kill in a few heartbeats.

He still held the lighter. He was ornery, and he still had enough left to thumb the wheel, striking flame.

There was so much gas lying splashed around, pools of it, that all that was needed to ignite it was to strike a flame.

Whoomp!

That was the coughing sound of the gas igniting. Blue flames spread outward from the hot point, an ever-widening disk.

The room was filled with flame.

Watching, Annie saw the back room fill with bright yellow light, which came pouring through the open doorway.

Then came smoke, in long serpentlike streamers.

Tongues of fire came licking out of the door frame. Flame spears lanced over the top of the partition walls.

The fire detonated the gas-filled jugs, unleashing a series of blasts. Shock waves bulged the walls, which would have fallen if the open ceiling hadn't allowed the main force of the blast to escape.

A fireball rose to the roof, mushrooming when it struck it, setting ablaze all that it touched.

Annie was a good distance away, but the first blast knocked her to the floor. When the last blast subsided, she rose, shaky, bruised, but otherwise unhurt.

Much of the store was on fire, and the blaze was spreading fast. She could feel the heat of it against her face.

At the center of the blaze was the back room, now an inferno.

Nothing could have lived through that holocaust. Not Pete. Not the ants; though Annie didn't know about them.

Annie coughed. The front of the store was fast filling with smoke. Time to go.

But not before she'd emptied the cash register, pocketing the take.

"Pete would've wanted it that way," she told herself.

The thought consoled her as she used the pay phone in the lot to call the fire department.

The feel of the cash stuffed into the pocket of her jeans consoled her even more.

15

AT ABOUT THE SAME TIME THAT UNCLE PETE'S Trading Post (and Uncle Pete, and the ants) was ablaze, Robbie Kellerman was eyeing his first hatchlings.

"Awesome," he breathed.

A dozen or so ants had emerged from their cocoonlike pupae. From the moment they came out of their shells, they were fully formed, active.

They were huge, the biggest ants he'd ever seen. Each one was wasp-sized. They seemed all jaws and stingers. The rear segment, the abdomen, or gaster, was shaped like a wasp's, from the tiny waist, to the oversized podlike shape, to the curved pointed tail ending in a needlelike stinger. The tip of the sting could be seen, while the rest was sheathed inside, held hidden until the time it would be used.

Robbie sat at his desk, the Ant Castle standing on the desktop. Nearby, a desktop lamp stood with its shade tilted, throwing light into the plastic cube. Robbie sat leaning hunched forward, peering down into the cube.

The ants crowded on top of the dirt, in the narrow space between it and the lid. They were active, excited. They were in constant motion, crawling on top of each other

Sometimes there would be a little tussle, as the ants tried each other out, jockeying for position. A pair would clash, wrestling each other. The smaller would quickly submit, backing off. There was some nipping with the jaws, but the stings never came out.

Their brains were pinhead-sized, but they had been programmed to keep the ants from killing each other. All ants in the colony had the same smell. That smell kept the stings from coming out. When they encountered another ant with that same smell, the kill instinct was suppressed, put on hold.

Any ant from outside the colony would lack the telltale scent, and be considered fair game.

Any living thing outside the colony was fair game.

In the cube, the ants were agitated. Perhaps they sensed the presence of the napkin-wrapped meat scraps that Robbie had smuggled away from the table, and that lay nearby.

This was the first real chance he'd had to examine them all day, since coming home from school. Dinner was done, Mrs. Cunningham was busy in the kitchen doing the dishes, and Gwen had gone out with her friends.

Robbie opened the napkin, taking a pinch of meat scraps between thumb and forefinger, holding it above the cube.

Clublike antennae waving, the ants raised up on their two rear sets of legs, clamoring for the food, jaws working.

Robbie lifted the lid of the feeding hatch. The ants milled below the opening, rising upright, reaching with their forelegs for the gateway to the outer world that loomed above them. The world of food, so tantalizingly close, yet out of reach.

Robbie sprinkled the scraps into the nest, showering the ants with meat. To their ant-sized frame of reference, the scraps were what sides of beef would have been to humans.

The difference was, if you dropped sides of beef on top of a man, burying him, he wouldn't be crawling out from under the pile so quickly.

While the ants shrugged off the masses of meat, then fell on them with mandibles working, tearing them apart.

Not eating them, they carried the scraps into the tunnels, to a chamber at the bottom of the nest.

The site of the future queen's chamber. The

colony hadn't produced a queen, not yet. But it would, soon.

Any female ant was a potential queen. That meant the vast majority of the colony, since there were few males.

It all depended on certain foods, hormone-rich secretions, which the workers produced in their own bodies.

Larvae fed this "food" would develop into queens.

Motion in a midlevel chamber in the nest caught Robbie's eye. The chamber was beaded with pupae.

As he watched, an ant squirmed headfirst out of the shredded end of one of the brown, nutlike pods.

It was wet, glistening, its antennae flattened against its upper body. The ant unfolded them, using them to probe its surroundings.

It was a big brute, a major. Warrior ant. Its jaws worked.

It began climbing upward, through the tunnels, toward the surface, where the food was.

In the chamber it had quit, another ant stuck its head out of a pupa, and began working itself out.

Throughout the nest, in every chamber, more ants were being hatched, right before his eyes.

They were big. And there were a lot of them.

"Cool," Robbie said.

For once, the ads hadn't lied. The reality of the ants was even better than the hype.

They were alien, exotic, hostile. Little monsters, in a mini-edition that he could control. Their armored bodies were a ruddy copper color, dark, sullen, like hot metal.

Big, too.

16

BY WEDNESDAY NIGHT, ROBBIE WAS GETTING worried.

Magic Instant Ants were no scam, no rip-off. Oh, no. In fact, they worked *too* well.

That was the trouble. Or part of it.

The other part was that the Ant Castle was a rip-off. Seated on the green-blottered desktop, it looked small, puny, like a novelty paperweight.

It was too small and flimsy to hold the mass of copper ants now filling it. And there were more coming every minute, literally.

A queen had been selected. She now occupied the lower chamber, laying eggs.

She was ten times bigger than the other ants, even the majors. She was as big as a grasshopper. Almost all of her was the egg-laying sac, a monstrously swollen gaster. The rest of her, the head and thorax and three pairs of legs, was ridiculously tiny in proportion to the sac, like a pilot squatting atop a blimp.

She kept laying eggs. That was what she did—that, and eat the food that the workers brought her.

Every minute or so she laid another egg. That's how it seemed to Robbie, who was nervously watching the copper pellets piling up.

The queen's chamber was the only one still holding its shape. The others had mostly collapsed, to one degree or another, crushed by the sheer weight of the ever-increasing ants.

Talk about overpopulation! The cube was as crowded as a free music festival.

The only reason that the queen's chamber was still intact, instead of buried under the weight of ants and dirt, was because groups of workers lined the curving walls, reinforcing them with their own bodies.

They were linked together, mandibles gripping their neighbor's legs, their own legs being likewise gripped. Like chain mail, or a chicken-wire fence.

A living structure, lining the domed chamber, a flexible framework able to support the weight of ants and dirt pressing down on it.

The cube was swarming with ants. Swarming.

The Ant Castle was a toy, unable to support a

colony of this size. All it consisted of was plastic squares, fitted into a snap-in framework.

It was bulging at the seams with ants. Was it his imagination or were the sides starting to curve outward, bending under the pressure of the fast-growing colony?

And those were just the ants that had sprung from the original egg cluster in the starting kit. What would happen when the new generation of eggs, laid down by the queen, began to be born?

Maybe the ants would eat each other. That would solve the population problem.

It'd be pretty cool to watch, too.

But he couldn't wait to see what would happen when the new eggs gave up their larvae. Which would be soon, as fast as the ants multiplied and developed.

The top of the nest, between the dirt surface and the plastic lid, teemed with a coppery lining, a mass of scores of ants in one seething pile.

When he fed them now, he had to be careful that none of them climbed over each other's backs, out the hatchway.

And the meat scraps he had pilfered weren't enough. The massed ants hit them like a shredder, tearing them up in less time than it takes to tell it.

He wouldn't like the ants to get loose in the

house, especially not in his room. There was no way that he could avoid getting tagged, rightly, as the guilty party.

The cube needed reinforcing. Working with a roll of duct tape, he tore off strips and pasted them down along the edges of the cube, strengthening it.

He picked up the cube so he could put some tape on the bottom. It hummed with inner activity, pulling off in its own direction, as if trying to get away from him.

It was like there was a spinning gyroscope in the cube.

The inner force was the ants, moving around, seething.

Once, he almost dropped the cube, catching it in the nick of time. His heart was beating fast.

He kept a good, tight grip on the cube while laying down the rest of the strips of tape. He put on more tape than he had planned, to make sure that the cube was really secure.

He thought the tape would hold. The strips were solid, blocking off about a third of the cube's inner space. He couldn't see what was going on in those parts of the nest.

But the ants couldn't get out.

Not yet, anyhow.

17

"ROBBIE, WHAT ARE YOU DOING?"

It was Thursday morning, early. Time for Robbie and his sister to get ready to go to school.

Robbie, fully dressed, was in the garage. It was a two-car garage attached to the house. In it was only one car, the other parking space being empty.

At one end of the garage was a roll-up sliding door, now closed. A few oil spots marked the smooth concrete floor. There was a lawn mower. There were snow shovels, a rake, a coiled green garden hose, a rack of garden tools, and some empty brown flowerpots. There were a couple of bicycles, a croquet set with some of the pieces missing, and a few folded lawn chairs.

At the far end of the garage, opposite the sliding door, in one of the long walls, an outer door opened on the backyard. Now it was closed.

In the upper half of the door were four panes of glass, covered with a gauzy curtain. The door faced east. Early-morning sunlight shone through the door windows, lighting the space. Beyond the light, there were cool gray shadows.

Opposite the side door, on the other side of the garage, was a connecting door to the house. At the foot of the door, two stone stairs led down to the cement floor.

The door was open. In the doorway stood Mrs. Cunningham, backlit by the glow of hall lights.

Diagonally across from her, on the other side of the garage, stood Robbie. He was facing a wall-mounted shelf unit, his back to the house door.

He'd been surprised by her sudden entrance. He started, looking back over his shoulder.

"Oh! Hi, Mrs. Cunningham. I didn't know you were there," he said.

"I'm sure you didn't," she agreed.

The wall unit's shelves were filled with the kinds of odds and ends that you might find in a garage.

His hands were busy below the waist, reaching into the shelves, doing something. She couldn't see what it was.

"What are you doing, dear?"

"Nothing, Mrs. Cunningham."

She went down the stairs, crossing to the side door. She stood beside it.

He turned, facing her, hands at his sides. His face was open, innocent.

"I was checking my bike, to see if I could ride it to school," he said.

The bicycles stood against the wall on the other side of the garage, opposite him.

"The bikes are over there," she said. Not accusingly, just pointing out a fact, as if she were correcting a slight mistake in grammar or pronunciation.

"I was looking for the air pump, Mrs. Cunningham. One of the tires looks kind of flat," he said.

That checked her. She tilted her head from side to side, peeking around him, trying to see the shelf area where he had been reaching.

From what she could see, nothing seemed odd or out of place. That was a disappointment.

Next, he tried to put her on the defensive.

"Are you looking for something in here, Mrs. Cunningham? Maybe I can help you find it."

She smiled thinly, her face bland. "No, thank you, dear. I wanted to make sure that the door is unlocked for the meter man. Your mother's note said that he was coming to read the meters today."

Which was true, as far as it went. A bank of utility meters was in place high on the rear wall, opposite the sliding door. On meter-reading days, the garage door was left unlocked for the utility-company man.

Now, as if to underscore the truthfulness of her story, Mrs. Cunningham unlocked the outer door.

Of course, she hadn't come in to do that, not really. A few moments ago she'd glimpsed Robbie sneaking into the garage, and had decided to investigate.

"Your breakfast is getting cold, Robbie." She motioned toward the doorway into the house, indicating that that was where he should go.

She pointedly waited for him to go first. He crossed the floor, climbed the two stone steps, and went into the house.

She followed, pausing in the open doorway, looking back. She couldn't see anything in the wall shelf unit that was out of place or out of line.

She'd take a closer look later.

Definitely.

Robbie was blank-faced, but his ears were burning. Inside, he was a knot of tension. His shoulders were hunched, as if waiting for a blow to fall.

Instead of poking around in the shelf unit, Mrs. Cunningham trailed him into the house, closing the door behind her, then locking it.

Although he tried not to show it, and was doing a pretty good job of hiding it, Robbie was scared.

Ants.

He hadn't slept much last night. He'd kept tossing and turning, waking up with a start. He'd lain awake in the dark, thinking that he could hear the ants moving around in the cube in the closet.

A house is never silent. At night, alone in the dark, in bed, you can hear it, because that's when you're listening.

Robbie had been listening. Each creak, groan, or thud, made by the house settling on its foundation, sounded like the ants cracking open the cube and getting free.

Gray light showed through curtained windows. Robbie had sat up in bed. For some time he'd been wide awake.

According to the bedside alarm clock, it was about five o'clock in the morning. There was enough light to see by.

Unable to wait any longer, Robbie had thrown back the covers and gotten out of bed. In pajamas, his bare feet cold, he went to the closet.

Ants.

When he'd put them away earlier, before

going to bed, they'd been more active, more frantic than ever. They were sullen, seething, their jaws snapping. They looked *mean.*

And hungry. He'd seriously underestimated the amount of food they needed. The meat scraps he'd smuggled from the table hadn't nearly begun to satisfy their endless appetite.

They'd gone to bed hungry. Hours later, at dawn, they could only be worse.

The lack of a light in the walk-in closet had never bothered Robbie before, until now. Even with the door wide open, it was dark, gloomy.

Standing on tiptoes, brushing up against clothes hanging from the rack, he reached for the overhead shelf. Moving aside boxes that he'd placed there for cover, he felt around for the cube.

It wasn't there.

That gave him a bad rush. Feeling around on the shelf, he found the cube, about six inches away from where he'd left it.

It couldn't have moved itself? It *had.*

Or, rather, it had been moved by the ants inside it. Their constant milling had caused it to move sideways. Had it moved forward instead, it would have fallen off the shelf, to the closet floor. That would have been fun, in the dead of night.

The cube hummed against his fingertips, vibrated by the ants within. They felt stronger than ever.

Holding the cube at arm's length, Robbie carried it into the fuzzy gray light. He groaned softly.

It was worse than ever. Even in the dimness, he could see the churning, throbbing ant mass.

The colony was a single being, about the size of a grapefruit. A copper grapefruit.

Nasty and starved.

Ants.

Fun was fun, but not when you were scared. They scared him. He didn't want them in his room anymore.

"What're they, crazy, selling people ants like this?" he said to himself.

The ants were crazy. Crazy mad. There were so many of them, he could hear them rattling around in the cube.

He had to get rid of them. Or at least, get them out of the house.

Mrs. Cunningham slept downstairs. To get out of the house, he'd have to pass by the guest room where she was staying. She was a light sleeper and an early riser.

Better not risk it.

He put the cube in a shoebox. An endless span of time dragged by, until sunrise.

Then it was morning, and the house began to stir, waking up.

Robbie watched for his chance. It was slow in coming.

First, Gwen was up and about, moving around in the hall. When she was finally out of the way, taking a shower, Mrs. Cunningham was awake and dressed and moving around downstairs.

Time passed and then breakfast was ready and Robbie was out of time; he couldn't wait any longer.

He picked up the shoebox, holding it to his chest. The cube slid around inside, thudding to a halt.

Robbie's heart started thumping. He went out to the landing, standing at the rail looking downstairs.

He went down the stairs, crossing the hall toward the front of the house. On his right was the archway into the kitchen, partially blocked by the corner of a wall.

Gwen and Mrs. Cunningham were in the kitchen. As he glided past, he turned to one side, hiding the shoebox with his body.

Then he was out of their sight lines. He didn't think he'd been seen, but he wasn't sure. He walked soft-footed, barely making a sound. Sneakers helped.

As it happened, he had been seen, by Mrs. Cunningham. She didn't miss much. She'd seen him flitting past. She was busy with a kitchen chore, so a moment or two passed before she was able to follow.

Robbie ducked into a hallway on his left. At the end of the short passage was the garage door.

He went into the garage, closing the door.

Ants. At least they were out of the house. They'd keep in the garage until later, when he got home from school.

Then he'd figure out what to do with them. Where to get rid of them. And how.

"It'd take a giant magnifying glass to burn these guys," he said to himself.

There were lots of hiding places in the garage, but most of them were closed to him. He was wearing his school clothes and couldn't get them dirty. Mrs. Cunningham would pick up on that right away.

He put the shoebox in the wall unit, in the corner of a low shelf. On the same shelf were some bags of potting soil, part of his mother's gardening supplies.

He put a bag on top of the shoebox, weighing down the lid. Another bag followed. It hid the shoebox pretty well, too.

Robbie had just finished up, and was rubbing some dirt off his hands, when Mrs. Cunningham had surprised him.

He'd fooled her pretty well, he thought.

In the kitchen, Gwen's breakfast stood untouched at her place at the table, while she stood nearby, chatting with one of her friends on her portable phone.

Robbie picked at his food. He was worried. Everything seemed okay, but one thought nagged at him. He wished he'd been able to give the ants a big feeding.

But he couldn't, not with Mrs. Cunningham around.

No way he could filch a snack from the fridge, sneak out to the garage, and feed the ants in the cube.

No time, either. In a few minuets he had to be out and on his way to school. Otherwise, he'd be late.

Not that he was so keen on feeding the ants. The last time he'd looked, they'd filled the cube up to the lid. He couldn't open the hatch to feed them, without them getting out.

They were hungry and mad. They'd be a lot more of both by the time he came home from school.

He was glad he'd put not one, but two bags of dirt on the shoebox. The ants needed to be pinned down in place.

They were hungry little devils.

18

MRS. CUNNINGHAM FOUND THE SHOEBOX. She went right straight to it, as if guided by radar.

Earlier, Robbie and Gwen had left for school. Mrs. Cunningham had cleaned the kitchen. She was one of those types who always cleans up immediately after eating. She couldn't abide a dirty dish.

When she was done, she went into the garage.

She'd been looking forward to the experience, savoring it like a kid with a sweet tooth waiting for dessert.

Robbie'd been up to some mischief. What? Something nasty, from the way he'd jumped guiltily when she'd surprised him.

Well, she'd find out what it was.

He'd been standing at the wall unit. There she went, peering into the shelf where his hands had been. It was low, below waist height. She leaned forward, squinting.

The shoebox, of course. It stuck out like a sore thumb. She didn't have to be a genius to see that the box was new, clean, and unmarked, except for a few fresh smudges from recent handling.

What was in it?

Contraband, no doubt. The forbidden.

A pack of cigarettes, perhaps. Or a can of beer, or a dirty magazine. Or worse.

"There's no limit to the nastiness of youngsters these days," she said.

She took off the bags of dirt, laying them beside the shoebox. She pulled out the shoebox with both hands. The top was dented from the weight of the bags, but still covered the hard paper box.

There was something inside. She took off the top of the box. Inside was the cube.

Whatever she'd thought she'd find, this wasn't it.

What was it?

She picked up the cube with one hand, hauling it into the light. She held it in front of her face, frowning.

The duct tape hid a lot of the cube from her view. She didn't know what she had, but she knew it was nasty.

In her hand, the cube . . . *moved.*

It heaved, swelling, as if there were a live eel squirming inside. *Something* inside that cube was alive.

Startled, she dropped the cube.

It hit the hard floor with a *crack,* breaking open.

The cube faces came apart, unfolding like a banana peel.

The ant mass broke loose, spilling across the concrete. An arrow-shaped copper column made straight for Mrs. Cunningham.

There was no hesitation. It wasn't in them. As one, the swarming colony superorganism raced toward her.

They were quick. Before she could react, dozens of warrior majors were scrambling up onto her shoes.

They climbed over her feet, ankles. Where they found flesh, they dug in and held on. They bit and stung.

Mrs. Cunningham reacted. She whooped and hollered, pumping her legs as if she were running in place. Her knees rose to her chest.

The ants kept coming, fastening around her like ankle bands. Biting and stinging.

Each sting was a white-hot needle being driven into her flesh. A knitting needle.

Each ant could sting ten times in a few seconds. Dozens, scores of ants, all stung at once.

Mrs. Cunningham got in some good screams,

but they were mostly muffled by the enclosed garage.

In this neighborhood, the houses were a good distance apart. If any of the neighbors heard the screams, they didn't think it was worth reporting to the police.

The screaming didn't last long.

Neither did Mrs. Cunningham.

Her legs folded at the ankles, spilling her to the floor. She flopped around like a fish out of water.

Now that she was on the floor, the ants no longer had to scale the giant, but could come at her from all directions.

The mega-dose of toxic ant venom pumped into her would have killed an elephant.

The horror was brief.

She was still alive when the ants fastened onto her face, but mercifully dead before they had finished eating her eyeballs.

It was about nine-twenty A.M. when Mrs. Cunningham died.

It took a few hours more before the ants finished eating her.

19

THE METER READER WAS SCHEDULED TO COME in the morning, but what with one thing and another, he didn't arrive until one in the afternoon.

His name was Joe. He parked the power-company van in front of the Kellerman house.

He had brown hair and wore the company uniform. He got out of the van. It was a warm, sunny day. He was hot in the uniform.

He started away from the vehicle, stopped, and went back to it. Inside, on the front seat, lay his cap. It looked like a bus driver's cap. It had a stiff, visorlike brim.

He put it on. Company rules. The higher-ups didn't like their workers to go around bareheaded. Except while driving, or indoors, field personnel were required to wear their caps at all times.

He didn't like it. His hair was thinning on top. He had a feeling, silly enough, but real to him, that the cap was causing his hair loss. The tight hatband cut off the flow of blood to his scalp, choking off the hairs, weakening them.

That's what he thought.

Clipboard in hand, he went up the driveway and around to the side of the garage.

It was a warm, lazy day. Birds chirped, bees hummed.

Not around the Kellerman house. Its surroundings were silent, deserted by the birds and the bees. They knew to stay away.

Not the meter reader. He was on automatic pilot. He didn't even have to think about what he was doing. His task was strictly routine, a monthly meter reading no different from all the many others on his route.

His mind was elsewhere, on last night's baseball game, on the weather, on his weekend plans, on how he was going to pay his bills, and on other matters, great and small.

He stood at the garage side door, the knob turning easily under his hand. The door was unlocked, as per the routine.

He opened it, stepping inside.

He was a couple of paces across the floor when it hit him: the stink, the mess, the filth, the acid reek.

Sprawled on the floor was a tattered bundle of

rags, wrapped around a clean-picked skeleton, all that remained of Mrs. Cunningham.

In her death spasms, she'd rolled partly under the car, and gotten wedged there.

Now she was rags and bones.

There were ants everywhere. He'd never seen so many ants in one place. Big ones, too.

Those he saw were only a part of the swarm. A small part.

Copper ants drizzled from above, falling on the floor. None fell on Joe.

He looked up. Hanging on the ceiling was a mass of about 150,000 ants, maybe more. It was the size and shape of an open beach umbrella, hanging point downward. The tip was only about twelve inches above Joe's head.

That was the main body of the ants.

Earlier, sensing the vibrations of pounding footfalls as Joe approached, the ants rolled up the walls and across the ceiling.

It was easy for them seemingly to defy gravity. They were a tree-climbing species. They were predators in all three dimensions: up, down, and sideways.

Why so many?

During the day, their numbers had multiplied many times their normal high-growth rate. The colony life cycle had gone into hyperdrive.

The ants were creatures of the world of

sixty-five million years ago. Through some fabulous freak of suspended animation, the dormant egg clusters had come alive, birthing the species into today's world.

Now, there's at least one thing new under the sun: the sun itself. Or, rather, the sunlight.

In the last half century, the earth's protective ozone layer has thinned, weakened. The layer acts as a barrier, screening out much of the sun's harmful ultraviolet rays.

The thinning screen lets more UV rays through. Already, they've begun taking their toll on certain radiation-sensitive life-forms, not least of which are humans.

All current-day life-forms are at least somewhat used to the increased UV, since it's part of the environment.

But the upped UV count was not a part of the environment of sixty-five million years ago. The hoplite ants had no defense against the increased solar rads.

The Kellerman house ants had had minor exposure to sunlight, during the times when Robbie had them out during daylight. But even the limited amount of light that had come through the windows into the room was awesome in its effect on Myrmex hoplites.

It was comparable to the situation of an albino, to whom the sun is poison, being stuck out in the middle of Death Valley at high noon.

The UV rays did more than give the ants the world's worst case of sunburn. Invisible rays sleeted through the ants, working on a microlevel, scrambling the DNA in their cells.

Result: mutation.

The colony life cycle had speeded up, like a film sequence run in fast motion. What would normally take days now took hours, as the eggs cycled through larva, pupa, and full-blown ant maturity.

New queens were born every minute, and soon began laying eggs.

Freedom from the cube had triggered the colony's growth phase.

Thanks to Mrs. Cunningham, there was plenty of food on which to feed and grow. For a while.

But the ants kept making more ants, and they were all born hungry. The colony had been getting ready to go into the active, swarm-raider phase when Joe made his timely entrance.

Timely for the ants, that is.

A mound of ants hanging upside down from the ceiling, above his head? It took Joe's mind a couple of split seconds before it could make sense of what it was seeing.

Namely, a mound of ants on the ceiling.

He knew enough to get out.

As if they sensed his muscles tensing, getting ready to make the big lunge for the door—and maybe they *could* sense it—the ants moved first.

As one, they let go of their hold on the ceiling.

They fell on Joe like a wet blanket. Wet with blood. His.

The ants went to work on him. He came apart, like a piece of meat tossed in a grinder. He went in whole, and came out chopped meat.

They ate him up, faster than the venom could kill him.

After a minute or two, he was a very sloppy Joe. All that was left was blood and scraps.

They ate those, too.

20

SPORTY RED MUSCLE CARS COST BUCKS. THE two McBane brothers could only afford one car. They had to share it, which sometimes created some thorny problems.

Now it was Gordy's turn to drive, and Duncan's turn to backseat-drive.

It was a little past three, on Thursday afternoon. School was out, the sun was shining, and it was time for fun. Funtime.

Gordy drove. Sitting beside him, in the front seat, was Helen Trent—or was that Ellen? Sometimes, like now, Gwen had trouble telling the twins apart.

Gwen sat in the back, with the other Trent twin, and Duncan. Duncan sat at the edge of his seat, leaning forward, thrusting his head over the top of the front seat.

"Watch out for that yellow car up ahead," he said.

"I see him, Dunc," Gordy said, steering around and past the yellow car.

"What's your hurry, Gordy?"

"I'm doing under the speed limit, Dunc."

"Seems faster."

"You're such an old woman," Gordy said, chuckling.

"I'm a safe driver."

"So'm I."

"Um."

"What, I'm not? Give me a break, Dunc!" He looked back over his shoulder at his brother.

"Watch the road, man!"

"I'm watching it."

"You should be more careful."

"Want to drive, Dunc?"

"Yes."

"Well, forget it. It's my turn, and I'm not giving it up," Gordy said.

Gwen sighed. "You're driving me crazy, both of you. I've got a solution: *I'll* drive."

"No way!" Dunc and Gordy shouted, in unison.

"I'm a good driver," she said, somewhat defensively.

The others smiled, some politely, some not so polite.

Gordy said, "The last time Mr. Mazuki had you for driver's ed class, he was so shook up that he had to take the rest of the day off."

"If he's that sensitive, he shouldn't be teaching driver's ed. It's not like I crashed the car or anything," Gwen said.

"Not quite."

"That is such a lie."

Gordy shrugged. "That's not what I heard."

"I'd like to know how these stories get started," Gwen said, indignantly.

The twin in the front seat put in lightly, "Don't pick on Gwen, just because she puts the car in reverse when she means to go forward."

"Once," Gwen said, her cheeks coloring. "I did that *once.*"

"I'm not picking on her," Gordy said. "I wouldn't let you drive either, Helen."

"Is that so?" Helen asked, a bit tartly.

"Yes."

"Hmmph!" She folded her arms across her chest.

In the backseat, Ellen put a hand on Duncan's arm.

"You'd let me drive, wouldn't you, Dunc?" she said.

"No."

She punched his arm, not hard. "You are so corny. I suppose you think that girls can't drive as well as guys, huh?"

"That's got nothing to do with it," Duncan said. " We wouldn't let any guys drive our car, either."

"None," Gordy agreed.

"This's our baby. Nobody drives it but Gordy and me." He eyed his brother suspiciously.

"And I don't much like him driving it," he added.

"Likewise, Dunc," Gordy said.

They were in Gwen's neighborhood, not far from her house. The red car neared an intersection, slowing.

From a different direction on the cross street came Robbie, walking fast. Intent on his own thoughts, he didn't see the red car.

Gordy said, "Hey, Gwen, isn't that your kid brother?"

"That's him. Could you stop for a minute? I want to tell him something."

"Sure."

The red car pulled up alongside Robbie, who had turned the corner and was now walking in the same direction as the car.

The car paced him, but he was oblivious to it.

"Out of it, as usual," Gwen said. "Honk the horn, that'll get his attention."

Gordy tapped the horn for a couple of beeps. Robbie looked at the car, seeing Gwen with her head stuck out of the window.

He slowed, halted. The car stood at the curb, beside him. "C'mere," Gwen said.

He went to the car, unhappy. "What do you want?"

"You're sure in a hurry."

"That's right, I am, Gwen."

"Ooh, the little man's in one of his moods."

"What d'you want?!"

"We're going on a picnic."

"So?" Robbie was intensely irritated.

"So, I won't be home for dinner tonight," Gwen said. "Tell Mrs. Cunningham, okay?"

"Okay!"

"You don't have to shout. You're in a nice mood today. Will you tell her?"

"I said I would."

"Good. Then I don't have to do it," Gwen finished happily.

She pulled her head back inside the car, sat back into her seat. "Bye," she said.

The car drove away. Watching it go, Robbie muttered, "Jerk."

"He's such a little creep," Gwen said in the car. "But it was lucky we saw him. Now we don't have to stop at my house so I can tell Mrs. Pest where I'm going, and have her get in my face.

"So, let's go to the park for our picnic," Gwen concluded.

"All right!" Gordy thumped a fist on the padded dash.

"Drive with both hands," Duncan said quickly.

"Will you lighten up? It's funtime!"

21

"PICNIC! BIG DEAL," ROBBIE SAID, PANTING.

He was heading home, moving fast. He was out of shape and short of breath. He wasn't the athletic type. His favorite sport was channel-surfing.

Exercise was alien to him. Still, he was moving as fast as possible. He was in a hurry to get home.

Ants.

He was hot and sweating. He wheezed, breath burning in his lungs. The few blocks that stood between him and home seemed to stretch out endlessly.

It was like one of those nightmares where you try to run, but you're stuck in slow motion. Meanwhile *something* is gaining on you.

Rubbery legs churning, he rounded a corner, finally coming within sight of his home street.

Parked in front of his house was a power-company van, a power-company utility pickup truck, and a couple of police cars. The police cars blocked the street, closing it to through traffic.

The police cars had their emergency lights on, flashing red and blue. No sirens.

A dozen or so cops were on the scene. Most of them were grouped around the cars. They stood facing the Kellerman house, watching it.

From the outside, the house looked perfectly peaceful and normal, no different from any other home in the neighborhood.

The cops didn't seem to think so. They stood around, clustered in small groups, tight-lipped, grim-faced. Most of them wore sunglasses, hiding cold, alert eyes.

They seemed to be huddled, making plans.

A small crowd of curious locals had collected. A couple of cops were keeping them back on the other side of the street.

Robbie sidled over to the group, coming up from behind. He was keeping a low profile.

A few newcomers added themselves to the fringes of the crowd.

"What's going on?" one said.

"Couple of power-company men went into that house and didn't come out," someone said.

"Why not?"

"That's what the power company would like to know. Not to mention the cops."

Another voice said, complainingly, "Why don't they do something?"

"They are. Looks like they're going in."

A pair of senior cops separated themselves from the others. They went up the driveway and around to the side of the garage.

Their guns stayed in their holsters. Violent crime was a nightmare that happened somewhere else, not here in quiet, peaceful Twin Oaks.

But where were the power-company men?

Earlier, when Joe, the meter man, had failed to answer the two-way radio in his van for a long time, the company had sent out two troubleshooters in a utility truck to investigate.

There was, as yet, no suspicion of foul play. Other drivers had gone out of radio contact before. Nine times out of ten, it was a case of equipment failure: radio, or vehicle, or both.

That's what the troubleshooters had expected to find when they followed Joe's scheduled route, tracking him to the Kellerman residence.

There was the van, parked in front, but no Joe. Both the van and the radio were working fine, no problem there.

So, the problem must be Joe. Where was he?

Maybe he had gone into the house, to use the phone to call in. Or maybe he was hobnobbing with the homeowners, joining them for coffee and cake.

One of the newcomers tried the front doorbell. It worked, but nobody came to answer it.

Maybe Joe was in the backyard, for whatever reason. Checking out a cable line, or something.

The other troubleshooter went around to the side of the garage, following the paved walk to the backyard.

On impulse, he tried the garage side door, finding it unlocked. He opened it, stepping inside.

There was a yell. The guy at the front door heard it, thinking his partner was calling for him.

He went around to the side of the house.

No partner.

"Now, where do you suppose he could have gone off to?" he said, wondering aloud.

"The garage, of course," he said, answering his own question.

He went into the garage . . . and went the same way as his partner. And Joe, and Mrs. Cunningham.

Into the devouring jaws and ever-hungry guts of an army of hoplite ants.

When the two troubleshooters failed to radio back to headquarters, the power company had called the cops.

Now here they were, on the scene.

The garage door was rigged at the hinges with a coiled spring device, which caused the open door to pull back, closed.

It was closed now.

One of the cops opened it. He must not have been as cool and undisturbed as he looked, since his hand was resting on the butt of a holstered gun.

He opened the door to hell, and it reached out and grabbed him.

The door swung open, its inner side lined with ants, covering every square inch of wood, massed five and six layers deep.

Peeling off the door in sheets, they wrapped themselves around the cop.

He went down screaming. He fell across the threshold, stretching facedown, half inside the garage, half outside.

The coiled spring device pulled the door back, but this time it didn't close. The cop in the doorway was blocking the way.

The door was ajar, half open.

Out came the ants.

Ants!

Like a flood of rusty water, they came surging out of the door, coming in waves. The cop in the doorway disappeared under a mass of them.

More followed, more, more, more. The wave

rolled out the door, flopping to the ground, fanning outward.

The second cop backed away, drawing his gun.

The first ants had already reached him, climbing up his shoes, over his ankles.

He roared, dancing a frantic jig. The head of the ant column swerved toward him, excited by his fear and pain.

It glided across the grass, like a wide, flat, coiling stretch of copper-red carpet that was rolling itself out.

And rolling up prey.

The dancing cop fired his gun into the spearhead of the column, pulverizing fist-sized chunks of ants.

Such gaps were only a drop in the bucket, instantly closed by the ever-increasing numbers of ants.

The cop tripped, fell. His gun clicked, empty.

The ants fell on him.

Soon they were full, and he was empty.

The garage emptied itself of ants, a quarter million Myrmex hoplites, hungry and on the prowl.

The colony was in swarm-raider mode.

The scene was chaos. Cops raced forward, their guns drawn, only to stop dead in their tracks when confronted with the damnedest thing they'd ever seen.

Handling an attack of prehistoric mutated swarm-raiding army ants wasn't part of the training at the police academy.

The cops hesitated, not the ants. To them, the cops were the same as everybody else.

Prey.

The copper-red tide rolled across the lawn, down the driveway, toward the cops.

Mystery monster or not, it was coming at them, and that was one thing that had been covered at the academy.

When something's coming at you with deadly intent, stop it. With deadly force, where needed.

The cops opened fire.

The crowd of onlookers flew in all directions, like frightened pigeons.

There was gunfire, gunsmoke, shouts, screams.

The shots had little effect on the column. It was like trying to stop a fast rising stream by shooting it.

Now some of the cops seemed to have blue uniforms with copper-red leggings. Copper-red leggings were not part of the regulation uniform. Especially not when they were woven from hoplite ants.

Once they cut your legs out from under you, and you fell, you were doomed. They were all over you.

A couple of furry, man-shaped forms were rolling around on the lawn, covered from head to toe with ants.

They stopped rolling fast. Stopped living, and went to the top of the hoplite food chain.

The surviving cops, about half the original number, fell back to the street.

The trouble was, even they already had some ants on them. Not many, a handful or two, but even a single ant could inflict agony with its strong jaws and tireless, venomous stinger.

Some shots went wild, blowing out the window of a nearby house, tagging an onlooker in the leg and dropping him.

A cop reached into the back of a police car, hauling out a shotgun. Another cop, blinded, screaming, ran into him, knocking both of them down into the street.

Where the ants were.

The two cops were swarmed. It was all over for both of them. With his last breath, the cop with the shotgun fired a blast at point-blank range into the car's gas tank.

It was no mistake. He knew what he was doing.

The gas tank blew up. There was smoke, fire, burning. Flames licked the tail of the car, good and hot.

The blaze set off a series of blasts, turning

the car into a fireball. The fire spread to another car.

Flaming gas pooled on the street, sizzling.

Across the street, crouching behind a lawn tree, peeking out at the blaze, Robbie could feel the heat of it on his face.

Inferno.

It served as a kind of fire break, holding back the ants. Incinerating those at the head of the column.

When enough of them had been destroyed, the column withdrew, retreating from the heat.

The fire was a threat, but they could always go around it. What they really hated was the stench of burning oil and gas, of hot metal and melting rubber.

Strange, alien scents, harsh and unnatural, the reek of technology.

That was unknown to them. Instinctively, they hated and feared it.

The column reversed, going up the driveway and around the side of the house, disappearing into the backyard.

Robbie decided it was a good time to make himself scarce.

He managed to hitchhike his way across the state line, into Pennsylvania, before the authorities picked him up as a juvenile runaway and returned him to Ohio.

Ohio investigators had a lot of questions

they wanted to ask him. He denied everything, playing innocent until he got hungry.

Then, for a bag of snack cookies and a glass of milk, he told everything he knew about his role in the onslaught of the Ants Who Ate Twin Oaks.

But that was later.

22

"ANTS," GORDY SAID.

He reached over to the picnic basket, plucking an ant off it. He held it between his thumb and index fingers, a small black ant. It squirmed, legs and antennae wriggling.

Gordy held it up, looking at it.

"Don't kill it," Helen said.

"I don't like ants getting into my food," Gordy said.

Gwen asked, "What's a picnic without ants?"

"Better," Gordy answered. He closed his fingers, squashing the ant.

Helen moved away from him. "You are so gross," she said.

He wiped his fingers in the grass.

Gwen said, "What'd you do that for?"

Gordy shrugged. "What's the big deal? It's only an ant."

"It wants to live, same as you."

"Then it should've stayed away from my

food. Hey, that piece of chicken you're eating wanted to live, too."

"They're dirty creatures, ants," Duncan said seriously. "All bugs are."

They were outside, in the picnic area of Stegg Park. In the center of a grove of trees were a few picnic tables.

Grouped around a table, drinking soda and eating sandwiches and pieces of cold chicken, were Gordy, Duncan, Helen and Ellen, and Gwen.

The grove was at one end of a patch of grassy fields that made up the park. There was a children's play area, with swings and a slide. There were enclosed tennis courts. There were jogging paths.

On a nearby rise was a parking lot, where the red car sat. At the top of the knoll was a frame metal power pylon, an Erector set–like tower carrying high-tension power lines.

It was part of a train of such towers, stretching across the landscape.

Sometimes you could hear the power lines crackle and buzz with electricity.

About thirty or forty people were using the park, scattered around it in small groups.

The picnic area looked down on a weedy lot. On the other side of it lay the backyards of a quiet suburban neighborhood.

Gwen's neighborhood. She couldn't see her house from here, but it wasn't that far away.

Duncan gazed in that direction, holding a hand over his eyes to shield them from the sun, which also lay in that direction.

From somewhere within that mass of trees and roofs, a line of smoke rose into the sky.

Gordy said, "What's happening there now, Dunc?"

"Not much. Things seem to have quieted down."

"There's still smoke. . . ."

"Not much. The fire must've played itself out."

Helen said, "Was it a fire?"

"What else?" Duncan said.

"It sounded like explosions going off, a little while ago."

Gordy said, "Probably some kids setting off firecrackers, getting a head start on the Fourth of July."

"Some head start. It's a month away," Gwen said.

"Oh, yeah? What do you think it was?"

"Probably my creepo brother blowing up the neighborhood." Gwen was joking, but in a sense, she wasn't far wrong.

Dunc said, "Whatever it is, it's done now. It's been quiet for the last ten minutes—"

Suddenly Gordy jumped up, electrified, roaring with pain.

"YEEEOW!" He slapped at his forearm, eyes bulging with agony. His thick neck was a mass of veins and tendons.

The others went to him. They were scared, shocked.

This was no joke, no prank. Gordy's fear and pain were evident in every part of his body.

"What's wrong?" Duncan whispered, wide-eyed.

"Something bit me!" Gordy was breathless, trembling. He eyed the smeared remains. Piercing deep into his flesh were the mandibles of the head of an oversized copper-red ant. They were still attached to the head, which was intact. The rest of the ant had been pulped by Gordy's slappings.

"An ant," he breathed, wonderingly. "An ant!"

Something crawled into view, climbing around the curve of his forearm, coming out from below the underside, where it had lurked unseen.

Gordy saw it. It was copper red, with two antennae and six legs. Big, too.

"Another one!" he shrieked.

Before he could kill it, it bit him. Then stung. It was the stinging that dropped Gordy to his knees.

"Gordy!" Duncan stepped forward, to help his brother.

Then it was Ellen's turn to scream.

She pointed at Duncan, who had moved past her, so that his back was now to her. "Y-your back, Dunc! It's covered with *ants!*"

He looked over his shoulder, down his back. A couple dozen hoplites clung to his clothes.

Ellen's fear rose to new heights as she saw an ant, sitting perched on the tip of her pointing finger.

It put the bite on her.

Her piercing scream rang in the treetops.

Excited, stimulated to the attack, the ants on Duncan fastened onto his flesh.

He reached behind his back with both arms, tearing at himself as if trying to rip out his spine. He spun, bellowing.

From the grass at the edge of the grove burst the spearhead of a hoplite column, swarming the picnic ground.

Fleeing the fire, the ants had gone in the opposite direction, through the Kellermans' backyard, down into a hollow, over a ridge, across the weedy lot, and into the park.

The grove became a place of horror.

The ants swarmed the youths.

Why not?

They were only human beings.

Prey.

Duncan went first. His thrashings carried him blindly into the middle of the column.

He fell, was engulfed, vanished.

From the first scream, Gwen had begun backing away from the others. As a result, she was the farthest from the column when it thrust its copper head out of the edge of the grass and into the grove.

"RUN!"

Somebody had shouted to run. Not Gwen. She was saving all her breath for running. She ran, hair streaming behind her, slender limbs flashing.

Trees flew past in a blur, echoing with screams.

The others were running. Gwen could hear them, running behind her. How many had gotten away?

Not Dunc. Only his blood was running. As the column had absorbed him, she had seen him coming apart at the seams.

It was a nightmare. If she should trip, fall, spraining an ankle, or breaking it—

The trees suddenly ended and she was breaking out into the open, on the flat near the parking lot.

Other people were running, too, fleeing the park, running up the knoll where their cars were parked.

They came from different parts of the park. The ants were attacking on a broad front.

The hard ground under her feet was sprinkled with copper ants. Gwen was tiring fast, but she changed course, angling away from the ants.

Sneakered feet slapped concrete as she stumbled into the parking lot. She staggered, almost falling.

People were running, screaming. Cars started up, racing away. Two cars crashed.

Gwen looked back, toward the grove. Gordy was close behind, stumbling, sobbing, but nearing the lot.

Farther back, midway between the lot and the grove, the twins came limping along. Helen was all but carrying Ellen—or was it the other way around?

Either way, the question became academic as the weaker of the two slipped and fell, dragging the other down with her, into and under the path of the ants.

Gwen choked, sobbing. Gordy staggered past, lurching toward the red car. His face was purple red.

Ant bites had swollen his hands into grotesque paws. He thrust one into his pants pocket, nearly fainting from the pain. He reached for his car keys, but his fingers weren't working.

The pocket tore at the edge, spilling the keys to the pavement. Gordy grabbed for them, missed.

Off balance, he fell down. He reached for them, crawling on his belly. His face was swollen like a toad's, bulging with boillike bites.

A copper limb surged into view, ribboning across the pavement, curving toward Gordy.

The ants had reached the parking lot.

And Gordy.

They blanketed him, starting at the toes and stretching to the top of his screaming head, in a few heartbeats.

Horror-struck, Gwen shook herself out of her daze as the column started for her.

She lunged for the keys, scooping them off the pavement just ahead of the tip of the column.

She went to the red car, the ants only a stone's throw away. They were a few paces away, before she found the right key and fumbled it into the lock.

She tore open the door and jumped inside, behind the wheel. The door slammed shut.

Was it antproof? She doubted it.

Her hand shook so much that she could barely fit the key into the ignition. The mighty motor started up like thunder.

Gwen threw it into gear and stomped on the gas.

The car shot backward, zooming away from the parking lot at high speed.

She meant to put it in drive, but she'd made a mistake and thrown it into reverse.

The car went off the pavement, onto the dirt.

A looming structure filled the rearview mirror.

Gwen hit the brakes. The wheels locked and the car skidded, sliding on dirt, fishtailing in reverse.

It rear-ended one of the legs of the high-tension tower. The leg crumpled, lamed.

Gwen rocked with the impact.

The motor stalled.

Metal creaked, groaned, squealed, and tore.

Weakened in one leg, the tower tilted. Power lines were pulled taut, twanging like giant plucked guitar strings.

Some snapped free and came slashing to earth. Those were live wires, juiced up with rivers of electric current.

The tower leaned some more, making an ungodly noise. Steel girders twisted, as easily as licorice sticks.

Gwen fought out of her daze. The tower was going to come down right on top of her.

Should she run? Sure, right into the ants.

She tried to restart the car. Nothing. She could have screamed. Instead, she remembered that the car was still set in reverse. She put it in park and tried again.

The engine fired up, shuddering the car.

Gwen put it in drive and drove away, angling to the left, on a course that would take her out from under the power tower.

Which was now falling.

The red car got clear of it. The tower toppled into the lot, crushing cars and people.

Severed power cables came down like whips, striking multiwatt blows on the writhing body of the ant column.

Electrocuting them. Most of them. But by no means all.

Gwen drove away. She kept driving until the red car ran out of gas, many miles from Twin Oaks.

She was safe. For now, at least.

As safe as anyone could be, in a world where devil ants, reborn, once more stalk the Earth.